The Speed of Light in Air, Water, and Glass

The Speed of Light in Air, Water, and Glass

LAURA SCALZO

ONE ONE TWO PRESS

Washington, D.C.

Copyright © 2018 by Laura Scalzo
All rights reserved. No part of this book may be reproduced in any form or by any electronic or mechanical means, including information storage and retrieval systems, without permission in writing from the publisher, except by reviewers, who may quote brief passages in a review.

One One Two Press
6412 Barnaby Street, NW
Washington, DC 20015

First Edition: October 2018

"Don't Imitate Me," by Matsuo Bashō, is in the public domain.

"A Kite is a Victim" by Leonard Cohen, collected in THE SPICE-BOX OF EARTH. Copyright © 1961 by Leonard Cohen, used by permission of The Wylie Agency LLC.

"A Carol of Harvest, for 1867," from *Leaves of Grass* by Walt Whitman, is in the public domain.

Library of Congress Control Number: 2018909839

ISBN: 978-1-7326940-0-2
ISBN: 978-1-7326940-1-9 (ebook)

Book design by Nita Congress
Cover design by Steve Campbell
Cover photograph by Anuski Serrano

Printed in the United States of America

for my dad

Don't imitate me;
it's as boring
as the two halves of a melon.

—*Matsuo Bashō*

Contents

Pilot Logbook

Stay or Go

Anatomically, I have the power of a fifteen-year-old girl of average strength and ability. Walking home from the Metro after dark, you may be able to make me give you my wallet, or worse. Atomically, I have the power of a star. If a star lets up on its regular work of nuclear fusion, it might fall to the will of gravitational collapse and implode into a black hole of energy so fierce it kidnaps anything stupid enough to get near it. Or it could go the other way, giving itself over to its own life force, its labor of nuclear fusion ramping higher and higher until it spends itself in a supernova explosion of color and light and scatters across the universe. I wonder, sometimes, if we have a choice in how our own body of matter will end up. On the days I think we do, I choose supernova.

CHAPTER ONE
A Long-Time Mad

'm driving downtown with a pack of people considered my family. It's so early it's the middle of the night. I like it. You can feel the city resting, taking a little break from the buses and tourists and congresspeople. Mom, her new husband, my somewhat recently hatched half sister, and the nanny are on their way to Reagan Airport. Not me. I'm on my way to the Hay-Adams hotel. Their plans don't include me and vice versa.

I'm a finalist in a STEM competition. I won a trip to Washington, D.C. I *live* in Washington, D.C., but that's okay because winning includes a week at a camp. Not a camp, *the* camp—otherwise known as the National Elite Science, Technology, Engineering, and Math Conference. There are five finalists including me. Over the week, we get to present our entries. My dad's here to watch and better yet, hang out.

My mom's elation is stratospheric. Take a bow, me. This never happens. Did I mention finalist? I did. Believe it when I say this particular piece of parental ear candy gave me a moment of weird and powerful hypnotic control over her. It also gave me a green light to not go on her vacation, a green light to stay with my dad over spring break, and a green light to register as a day camper—sorry, day *conferencer*—instead of a dorm dweller. It was a supernova's worth of green lights.

We pull up to the hotel. My dad's out front, track pants, PENN sweatshirt, bare feet, and hair straight out of bed. His arms are across his chest with his hands under his armpits, thumbs in front. He lifts up one foot then the other as he talks to the doorman who's dressed the exact opposite, in a formal uniform and a big heavy coat.

My mom and my dad haven't spoken since they signed the divorce papers somewhere around my first birthday. She's never said the words but she despises him. Even now she won't look but she forces herself, just for a second. No way she's leaving me at the door of a hotel in the dark morning without laying eyes on him. He waves—respectfully, I think. She's doing her ice queen thing. It's not an act when it comes to him.

The doorman takes my big suitcase and backpack. I kiss the half kid, Mom, Dave, even the nanny, and I'm gone.

Nope.

There's a *dink, dink, dink* of Mom's ring on the car window. I turn back just enough to see her mouth *Julia*, her forehead serious and fearful. She gives me the *text me* sign, finger tapping opposite hand. I give her the *I love you* sign. I'm not promising anything.

And so it begins, the deluxe combination of my dad, my science, my city, the luxy luxe luxe Hay-Adams hotel. We have hugs, we have breakfast at the big table in his suite, we have bang-bang rapid-fire father-daughter science and whatnot talk.

And so it ends. He can only stay one day.

My day conferencer status evaporates. He informs me that I'm to be a resident camper assigned to a George Washington University dorm room. Showers down the hall. Wear flip-flops so you don't get fungus. The gut punch of this reality is the intersection of wanting to lay my head on the table and weep and reach across my plate and strangle him.

I swallow it whole.

We have a day and a night. I'll take it, but he needs to pay. Not in money, but in sorry.

I look around the suite where I won't be staying, long and sad, just to rub it in. It's huge, with sofas, a desk, everything; we even have our own rooms. I turn to my dad and smile, but my eyes say *pay*.

He smiles back and says, "I spy with my little brown eye, something white."

"The White House." The White House is outside our window, across from Lafayette Square.

"Yes."

It's my turn. "I spy with my little brown eye, something white."

"The Washington Monument."

Right, the big pointy pencil is right behind the White House. This is the baby version of a game we've been playing forever.

"I spy something toile," my dad says, bringing it up to present-day challenge level.

"The wallpaper, the rug, the pattern of the walks in Lafayette Square, the statues, the sky." I don't know what toile is. He shakes his head at each guess.

"The drapes in your room and the headboards and that thing that goes around the bottom of the beds," he says.

I can see the fabric he's talking about through the open bedroom door. It's old-fashioned scenes in dark beige on a light beige background.

"How do you even know what toile is?" I ask, though I know the answer, his girlfriend's a decorator.

He shrugs. A lie.

"I spy something silver," I say.

"The flower vase, the tray, the coffee pot, the knife, the fork, the spoon, the pen and holder on the desk."

I shake my head at each guess. "The Air Force Memorial." I point in the direction of the three silver arcs far out on the horizon in Virginia. You can't see it but we both know it's there. The game has a hypothetical element to it.

"Good one," he says. "I spy something pink," he adds right away. We're moving into the speed round.

"Cherry blossoms." We can't see these either, not from our window, not from anywhere. Even though it's early April and they're supposed to be here, they're not. It's too cold.

"No."

"Jefferson's pink underpants."

"Yes."

I'm long grown out of underwear jokes. He should know this, but we've been going to the Jefferson Memorial every April my whole life. It's always the same, first we look out over the Tidal Basin and admire the pink ring of cherry trees surrounding it and then we turn and go up the steps. When we're inside and standing in front of Jefferson, he asks if I know that he wore pink underpants. When I was little, it was to make me laugh, but now it's tradition. After the underwear joke, he reads the words that circle the inside of TJ's marble hut, *I have sworn upon the altar of god eternal hostility against every form of tyranny over the mind of man.* Then he says, "Eternal. Hostility. That's a long-time mad."

For now, we leave the breakfast dishes on the big table and head over for our annual visit, because why wouldn't we? When we get there, a gray wind is pushing everyone around. The Tidal Basin is a small choppy sea. The paddleboats are closed. The cherry trees don't have a single blossom. I'm sure they know what they're doing, but I'm worried about them. I don't know if they're fragile or strong.

Following the standard visiting procedure, my dad takes the obligatory shot of me on the top step, Tom hovering in the background. I want to refuse to smile, but I don't. I've never not smiled for this picture, though all the other years it was because I was happy.

Back at the suite my dad says, "We're going to have to get you signed up for that dorm."

"Yes," I say and radio *pay me* eyes, but he doesn't receive.

Mom signed me up on the phone. We call and the recording says go online. We set up an account to change my status. The password is Fractalgirl15. My status as day conferencer is officially over. I am a dorm resident. I'll have a roommate whose feet smell and goes through my stuff while I'm sleeping. I just know it.

It's not far to GW—I can even walk—but in the morning when we say goodbye in front of the hotel, my dad puts me in a cab and signals for another one. He's going straight to the airport to get to where he needs to be. I never even asked where that was.

I tell the driver to take me not to George Washington University but to the Lincoln Memorial. I pull out my phone, sign into the camp account, and change my finalist status from *Resident* to *Not Attending*.

CHAPTER TWO

A Boy Asleep at the Vietnam Veterans Memorial

braham Lincoln's got my back. Well, he's behind me. I'm on the top of his stairs looking out. I had to *kalunk, kalunk, kalunk* my big rolling suitcase all the way up, plus my backpack's pretty heavy. Worth it. It's a good view. The perfect rectangle of the Reflecting Pool stretches out long toward the Washington Monument. It's the same gradation of red to orange to yellow as the sky. The double image of the Washington Monument is the laid-down reflection and the real standing-up thing.

My dad thinks he knows where I am. So does my mom. He'll need proof of where I've been, eventually. My mom will need proof immediately. I take a picture of the sunrise and write, At Lincoln with Dad. Then, Scattering is light waves hitting molecules and particles in the air. It's why the sky is blue. When the sun is low on the horizon, light has to travel farther and the short-wave violet and blue light is too scattered to see. That's why you see other colors, the long-wave ones. I text it to my mom.

And just like that, with a soothing sciency lie, my phone, after years of being an umbilical cord, disconnects me. I beam a false signal to the satellite hovering overhead and my message is not a link but a force field, my very own personal nuclear weapons shield. It zigzags me with freedom and fear.

Mom texts back immediately, Beautiful. Have a great week. Make sure there's video of your presentation. Love.

Ohhkaaay. Not sure how that's gonna happen.

There's a bunch of people milling around, looking out over the mall, up at Abe. A woman with black hair, straight and long under a leopard-skin hat, comes up to me. "Would you take a picture of our group?" she says, handing me her phone.

This happens a lot. I've shot a pack of Brownies in front of the Bill of Rights, two old ladies in front of the Chuck Close painting of Bill Clinton at the Portrait Gallery, Chinese tourists ice skating in the Sculpture Garden, you name it. I have a face that says I'm not going to steal your phone or your camera. I've been meaning to get started on looking more dangerous for a while now.

There's a lot of conversation in Spanish, which I only half understand. The lady with the leopard hat organizes them in front of Abe, positioning everyone around a young guy—older than high school, but not much. They're all squeezing against him. He's trying not to let on that he can't breathe.

I step back to get them all in the shot with Mr. Lincoln, and give them the flat palm for hold it.

"Cheese." Saying it makes *me* smile. I take a few shots. They look happy. I feel useful.

The group begins breaking up and I see that the guy they were crowding around has legs made of metal.

I hand the leopard lady her phone.

"My son is home," she says.

I don't know what to say, "*No vaya al zoo,*" is what comes out. Don't go to the zoo.

She frowns but right away sees that I'm talking about her hat. She touches it and says, "The leopard will fall in love with me!"

I nod like a crazy person.

They're leaving, saying *gracias* and *thank you*, softly so as not to disturb anyone, even though it's only me.

"*De nada.*"

The lady smiles at me, "*Son usted solo?*"

Am I alone? I understand that.

"*No, tengo una familia,*" I say. I have a family.

She gives me a weird look like what am I doing hanging around Lincoln at this hour. I could ask the same of them, but I know.

I *am* alone. But you know what? Nothing bad happens at Lincoln. That's why I came here. No one's ever done anything but sung songs about peace, spoken up for civil rights, or felt the greatness of Lincoln whose face and words tell you that the dead would not die in vain, he would see personally to it.

But here's this guy with his legs gone and a whole family of people who don't understand he can't breathe. And here's me and my only problem is my mom hovers like a maniac and my dad can't find the time to stick around, which I know doesn't compare, but still.

I walk down the steps, slowly kulunking my suitcase behind me. The long-wave colors are receding. I want my dad here. I want that guy to have his legs back.

If my dad were here, we'd walk over to the big statue of Albert Einstein. We're fans. I decide to go without him.

Near the low black V of the Vietnam Wall, I stop to look at a pile of desert camouflage khaki and puffy neon orange. People leave stuff at the Wall all the time, but this is pretty big. Two cops are coming up from the deepest part, where the sides come together. They're almost to the pile when it unfolds, reverse-origami style, into a living, breathing boy. The cops step back as he stands up, then move forward fast.

"I fell asleep, I fell asleep." The boy is shouting and trying to move his arms, but the cops have a grip on him. They look over at me, stop what they're doing, and stare as if I'm the one breaking the law. I mean the kid is getting arrested. What are they looking at me for? They must have the same thought because they go back to what they were doing, the boy struggling, them restraining.

"Do you have a name here?" the lady cop says. It sounds like she's asking him his name in an odd way but she's asking if he has a name on the Wall.

"Is there a name?" she says again.

"Michael Kovac."

The cops look at each other. "Is that who you're trying to find?"

He doesn't answer.

"Now come on son, we'd like to help."

This is the kind of police help my mom is always talking about. "As your mother and a lawyer, let me tell you something," she's said a million times, "never, ever talk to cops."

"Air Force Captain Michael Kovac," he says.

"All right." The cop holding him from behind lets his hands drop so the boy is just standing there on his own. "He was in the War?"

"Yes, he was a pilot, he went to Vietnam but he didn't come back. He isn't home and he isn't here. Why is that, why is that?" He's shouting again, but it sounds more painful than dangerous.

The guy cop pats him on the shoulder and tells him to take it easy. Then the weirdest thing happens. They look back at me and, with a kind of ushering motion, indicate they're entrusting him into my care. Or maybe it just seems that way because the boy picks up his backpack and walks right past me.

They look up at me again. I want to put my arms out and yell, "What?" but I stand still. They turn around and slowly walk back down to the deep center of the Wall and up the other side.

I don't want them to change their minds, have them come back and ask questions, so, keeping cool, I roll my suitcase down the path, pick a random spot on the Wall and stare at it.

I don't know anyone who died in the Vietnam War. I'm pretending.

You look at the black polished stone and see yourself. You read the names on the wall and they're on you. That's how it is at the Vietnam Veterans Memorial. I stare at my reflection. How can I be part of something that happened before I was even born? I look away. The cops are gone. The boy is gone.

THE STATUE OF ALBERT EINSTEIN is big, really big, but not all formal like Jefferson and Lincoln; he's hanging out, relaxing. I climb up and sit on his lap. What a baby. I have a picture of my dad and me in this same spot from a year ago, but I've changed too much to beam it to my mom. I take a shot of the page Albert's holding with his famous equations on it and write, Einstein Statue. I don't write anything else. Suddenly dazzling my mom with science feels like monkey tricks and I don't want to do any. My dad would like this snap too, but the idea of a virtual father-daughter moment instead of the real live one we're supposed to be having jabs my heart.

I close my eyes, trying to breath out my bang-bang jabby heart and breath in Einstein's absolute and reassuring equations.

I fill my brain with the image of my Cassiopeia A. Cas A is what's left of a supernova that blew up eleven thousand light years from earth; its smithereens showed up here three hundred years ago in a wild burst of colorful light. My Cas A takes up a whole wall of my room and I never get tired of looking at it. Thinking about it makes me feel better.

I open my eyes and there's a boy standing in the center of the scale universe mapped out on the big platform that Albert sits on. The same boy.

"It makes an echo," I call out, playing the informative tour guide to counteract getting caught sitting on Einstein's lap, breathing out anger and breathing in math and supernovas.

"KAL KOVAC," he shouts and nods approval when it echoes. I nod back.

He takes a step toward my suitcase and backpack, which I'd left near Albert's giant foot. "Coming or going?"

I jump down to grab them.

"I'm not gonna steal your stuff," he says, super huffy.

"Not coming or going. Just out walking my pet tarantula." I put a foot on my suitcase. I can be huffy too, especially when I'm nervous.

He's tall, around my age. He has one white eyebrow and one reddish brown, the same color as his hair. I noticed it when he walked past me at the Vietnam Memorial but didn't quite believe it. Now I see it's true. His eyes are brown and annoyed. "I'm not gonna steal your stuff," he says again.

"Okay, okay."

"He in there?"

"Who?"

"Your tarantula."

"Yeah. Except he's a she."

"Does she know?"

"That she's a she?"

"No, that she's being walked."

"No, but I do."

"Does she know how to get to Union Station?"

"No, but I do." I point toward Union Station and just kinda start walking.

"Food?"

"Crickets, grasshoppers…small ones."

"Not her, me."

"Um, so, yeah."

The logbook got wet from my leaking windshield. I was back at the base for repairs and the supply officer saw it and issued me this one.

It was hot enough to where a couple of guys thought they should try and fry an egg on the wing of a plane, which they did and ate. That's what got me to figure I'd try drying out the old log. It'd either burst into flames or be good as new. Ended up being fine so I thought I'd hang onto this book and use it for a place to keep track of myself.

Been doing a lot of personnel transport, mostly Udorn to Saigon, but lately been at Vientiane some and Long Tieng some too. Both places lousy with CIA, who, no doubt, read any mail I would post.

CHAPTER THREE

The Emerald City But Granite

Vendors are setting up their trucks on the sidewalk. They aren't open yet, but I talk one of them into selling me Cheetos and Nerds Rope—as luck would have it, my favorite candy in the whole wide world. I give the guy a twenty and he just looks at my hand when I put it out for change. There's a premium for off-hours transactions.

My mom gave me two hundred dollars for my week at camp. I'm sorry to see that twenty go. I don't know what's going to happen, but I'm anticipating needing money.

"Want to see?" We had walked up Constitution Avenue and were in front of the big stairs of the National Archives. I don't wait for an answer, but start, for the second time this morning, kalunking my suitcase up a huge set of steps.

At the top, it's the porch of a giant. The columns are as big as redwoods; the landing is long and wide and leads up to the largest set of doors on earth—that's a field trip fact, not just me exaggerating.

Big pink banners announcing the Cherry Blossom Festival hang down between the pillars. I sit on the top step, underneath one of the banners. Kal sits opposite me and leans against a pillar. We pretend to stare out at the city waking up, but we're really sneaking glimpses at each other—well, me at him anyway.

He's a bunch of bony angles. When he pushes his hair back, which he does a lot, there's a matching white streak above his white eyebrow.

I throw him a bag of Cheetos.

"Nothing better than eating Cheetos within earshot of the Declaration of Independence," I say, jerking my thumb toward the doors to the giant's house.

"The 'We hold these truths to be self-evident, that all men are created equal, that they are endowed by their Creator with certain unalienable Rights' Declaration of Independence? That one?"

"Yeah that one, that's pretty good, can you do any more?"

"Nah, I don't even know what that means."

"Well, it's saying that…"

He waves me off. "I know what it's saying, what *I'm* saying is that I don't know what it means."

"Well, you grew up in this country and you grew up free, didn't you?"

He stares, like he's trying to decide if he despises or pities me. "What are you, eight?"

"What's that supposed to mean?"

"Do you buy all this?" He swoops his arm to indicate the Capitol, the museums and monuments, the government buildings.

"No, I don't. It's a pile of crap. It's the Emerald City but granite, run by not one giant fake but a whole freaking bunch of them. Except for this place. I mean, I like the Declaration of Independence, the Constitution, the Bill of Rights. I buy it, yeah. Yeah, I do." I point across the street to the National Gallery. "Some good stuff in there, too."

"Like what?"

"Van Gogh's green face, Degas's ballet dancers. I also like the big painting of Walt Whitman at the Portrait Gallery. That's good. I like Walt, and I like the building. It was the Patent Office, then it was a Civil War hospital, and now it has all this cool art and stuff. Lincoln liked to rummage around in there, look at all the inventions—he was a patent lawyer, right? That was before the war. Then it was a hospital. Walt Whitman would go there to help the soldiers. Now you can see his portrait, right there in the same place. So, yeah, I like that."

A cop looks at us from down on the sidewalk. Kal sits up like the guy might tell us to get moving, but I stay put. I know my rights—I mean, they're right behind these doors.

When Kal finishes his Cheetos, he smooths out the bag, pressing it against his thigh. He folds it several times until it's a small square and puts it in his pocket. He opens his Nerds Rope carefully, pulling the wrapper apart at the seam, then flattens and folds that too.

"My grandfather disappeared," he says. "He was a pilot in Vietnam, but he never came home. He's not on the Wall. He's not POW. He's not MIA. He's gone. The U.S. government says he came home, but he didn't come home."

He looks at me as if I, with my ballet dancers, Lincoln, Declaration of Independence, and Walt Whitman might side with a United States Government that did not return his grandfather home from the war.

"How long have you known he wasn't on the Wall?"

"Since it was built, but I had to see for myself; I'm going to have to pick up where Suzy leaves off." He's giving me the facts like a pile of bricks for me to hold, and then stops and looks at me like maybe I'm too weak to carry them.

"I have something. Proof," he says. He opens his backpack. He takes out an envelope wrapped in a Ziploc bag and hands it to me. "This is the last letter she ever got, but there wasn't a letter, just the envelope. There's a message on the inside though, in pencil. It's written so lightly she almost didn't see it. It says, *These boys say fly until you die but I'll be home soon.*"

I hold the envelope carefully, understanding I'm not to remove it from its protective Ziploc. In blue ballpoint pen it says, *Suzy Kovac, Hedge Apple Farm, Sydney, Ohio, 45365.* There's no return address.

"Hedge Apple Farm. Is that where you live?"

"Yeah." Kal's mouth is a line.

"Can you eat them?"

"What?"

"Hedge apples."

"No. They're these big green things."

"For?"

"Throwing at cars, duh."

"That how you spend your time?"

"Just the one time." He smiles. "I was little but Suzy doesn't mess around. I built a catapult though, after that. It could really make them fly—just not at cars. She thought that was cool. Creative or whatever. What's the point in having all that ammo if you can't launch it?"

"Good thing they don't give you the nuclear codes."

"Yeah, good thing." He laughs.

"Suzy is…your mom?"

"No, my grandmother. I'm with her. My mom's not doing too well. She's kinda lost it. She's kinda gone. She is gone. We don't know where she is. No dad I know about."

Kal looks out across the city and says, "If I find my grandfather I can…fix it. I think she'd come home. My mom. I think she'd see it was safe. That's what I think."

"Where are you going now?"

"Home. Maybe not."

So Suzy, this is for you. In case I forget, or something happens, I want you to know I was here and who I was here and what I did on the other side of the world from you, and that I thought of you every day, and over everything, I love you best.

What a man that loves a woman this much is doing so far away from that woman I don't know. As much as I am a citizen of the United States of America I am a citizen of your heart. I try not to think too hard about what that means, but figure get this thing done and come home.

Before we know it, I'll be coming down County Highway, a speck moving in the distance through waves of summer heat and then a truck pulling into the farm road and then a man knocking and calling through the screen door. You'll come running from somewhere in that cool shady house and it will be how it's always been, two people with and for each other, but more because there will be Elizabeth and I will introduce myself to her, say it's her dad, and I will never introduce myself to her again.

CHAPTER FOUR

Fractals, Kites

'm named after a fractal. A Julia Set. That's on my dad. Our last name is Bissette. Julia Set. Julia Bissette. My mom didn't even know. He just insisted, and she, for the one time in her life, relented. I love this. Tension and subversive tactics from day one. Rock on, people.

A fractal is a thing that's itself over and over again, forever. Think of it like looking at your own self in a three-way mirror. Fractals are a way to describe things that are impossible to describe. You can draw a circle with geometry, but you can draw a snowflake with fractal geometry. Fractals are the science of jagged edges.

You can make fractals on a computer with a simple program or you can draw one with paper and crayons. Like the way you drew a tree in kindergarten: Start with the trunk, that's the first iteration, draw two lines off of that, that's the second iteration, two more lines off of each of those is the third iteration. You can make as many iterations as you want for as big and dense a tree as you want. Ta da, a fractal.

Parents, name your kid Algebra and someday they will whisper that lovely word STEM to you. Okay, not really, but I'm sure some of you will try it.

Fractals are the most interesting thing on the planet. I worked on mine all the time. I did it instead of my homework. There was pushback, which is why my mom's "I have a STEM child" pride is so annoying. They're mine, not hers.

I'm not in the habit of telling too much to strangers, but I tell Kal about my fractal and the camp/conference. He looks at me so weird, I elaborate. "It's a competition. There's a prize for the best one. Money."

He starts to say something, then stops. I can't tell if he thinks I'm brave, stupid, or too much of a freak to bother with.

"What else do you do besides catapult hedge apples?" I say, to change the subject.

"Help with the farm some, work on my kites. I have a lot of kites. Fifty-three. Fifty-three kites so far."

"How come so many?"

"Flight. Math over gravity. You have these equations, lift against weight," he moves his hand up and down, then side to side, "thrust against drag. It uses opposite forces. The truth of it can't be bought or sold or stolen. It's an…unalienable right."

"Guaranteed by?"

"Not the Declaration of Independence, I'll tell you that much. My mom, when I was little, before she…before she left, used to say this kite poem at night, instead of a lullaby. Not the whole poem, just part of it, except for once. So kites are, you know, what I do now, and how I remember then."

"Did you make all those kites?"

"Some—a lot actually. I bought some, and some were presents. I got the first one the day I was born. I guess you could say I've been collecting them my whole life."

"You got a kite when you were born?"

"Yeah, there was a Japanese family that lived near us. The man came to the U.S. to work at the Honda plant. He didn't run it but he was pretty high up over there. Suzy told me he used to come to the farm because he had grown up on a farm and he missed it. In Japan, they give the firstborn son a kite, so he gave me one. Suzy and my mom hung it over my crib. It's still over my bed…" He trails off.

If he thinks I'd make fun of him for sleeping under a kite, he's wrong.

"It's made from paper and bamboo. The artwork on it is like nothing you've ever seen."

I want to remind him that I'm acquainted with the National Gallery of Art, but I don't. I want to hear about his kite, though I doubt the artwork on it's like nothing I've ever seen.

"It's a picture of a boy, Kintaro. He's from a Japanese fairy tale. When he was a baby, his mother had to flee to a mountain cave, so he grew up wild in the forest. He's brave and really strong. There's also a carp jumping out of the water. Carp are brave and strong too because they have to swim against the current to lay their eggs. So that's my kite, my first one."

He's shy for a moment, then says, "I made a kite for Nicholas McGill!"

"What!" Nicholas McGill is the star of the Pittsburgh Penguins, archrival and polar opposite of Ilya Avilov, our guy for the Caps.

"Yeah," he laughs.

"You made him a kite?"

"When he was out all those games from his concussion, for a get well present. I wanted him to be skating again so bad I couldn't stand it, so I made him a kite. It was black and gold, a fighting kite. I sent it to him, and I sent him a note about kite fighting and that I hoped he would be back on the ice real soon."

"What's kite fighting?"

"You battle with them in the sky. He wrote me back. He told me that Nova Scotia, where he's from, is a good place for kites and how much he liked the one I sent him. He said by the time you get this letter, you will have heard that I'm cleared to play. And it was true, the news came out the day before."

I picture Nicholas McGill flying his fighting kite by the ocean in Nova Scotia, the freezing North Atlantic air coming off the water, cutting through, but him not noticing. He grew up there, he had a kite. And for a minute I fall in love with him. I fall in love with Nicholas McGill. Nick McGill, the Pens captain who I've booed with all my might and made fun of for having a head made of glass!

I look at Kal—Kintaro, brave and strong, raised in the mountain forest—and ask him the question I've been afraid to ask. It's about Mike Kovac. His isn't a war story I understand from school and field trips, a Civil War soldier breathing his last breath, Walt Whitman holding his hand at the Patent Office, not even a mile from the White House and President Lincoln himself. "Is it possible that your grandfather didn't want to fight the war anymore and he beat it out of there? I mean, how can you be sure?"

Kal stands up, picks up his backpack, and walks down the steps.

"Wha…where are you going?" I call after him. "I'M SORRY!" I yell.

He throws his hand up without looking back.

I stand up.

"HEY! I'M REALLY SORRY!"

He crosses over to the other side of the street and walks up Constitution Avenue until he's out of sight. I stare and stare and stare lost in… what? Not thought, I'm not thinking anything, just lost. I look down. I'm still holding the envelope in a Ziploc bag. *Suzy Kovac, Hedge Apple Farm.*

I stand under the bright pink banner waiting for him to come back. When he doesn't, I pray. It's not even a prayer, but it's the only one I know. *Energy equals mass times the speed of light squared, energy equals mass times the speed of light squared, energy equals mass times the speed of light squared.*

Laos is a real kingdom, with a Royal Palace and King and Queen and Princes and Princesses and a sleeping giant too. There's unrest in the land but the king only wants peace. Why wouldn't he? He's king!

It's a landlocked dog of a country, set in the crook of the arm of Vietnam. Its secret is the Ho Chi Minh Trail, a supply route through the jungle that connects the bitch mother's tilted head to her cradling arm—the lifeblood of the North Vietnamese Army.

Laos is a neutral country—neither communist nor democratic—a friend to all, the Switzerland of Southeast Asia. Their promise to the world is peace, but there is no peace.

The United States and the Royal Family and the South Vietnamese Army and General Vang Pao, the great leader of the Hmong mountain tribe are at war with the Communist Pathet Lao and the North Vietnamese Army here in the Kingdom of Laos. I write the truth to myself and someday to you, Suzanne, though I am sworn not to say it. We are at war in Laos. So much is happening that can't be told; even in Saigon, we're a rumor no one quite believes.

CHAPTER FIVE

The Hay-Adams Hotel Again

This morning's breakfast comes with the *Washington Post*. I'm reading it, propped up on puffy pillows against a toile headboard. There's Frosted Flakes in a pretty white bowl with a matching mini pitcher of milk on a silver tray next to me. I spy something white. I spy something silver.

I couldn't go home. Someone's there, watching the house and taking care of Avilov—our dog Avilov, not the Caps' Avilov. I couldn't go home, so I decided to come back here. I called up and asked the woman who singsong answered, "Hay-Adams, nothing is overlooked but the White House," if there was anything available. When she said yes, I told her Stuart Bissette would be extending his stay but would like to use a different credit card. I did this all in my best imitation of my mom on work call—friendly-ish and efficient with a trace of demanding. A room was available. I used the credit card my dad gave me two years ago and told me never to use. I suppose I'll find out what that means, if anything. It hadn't expired, the card or my father's test, if that's what it's been. Lucky him. This could be the solution to the problem of his owing me.

Still, I was nervous. My heart pounded in my ears as I read the numbers.

"And the name on the card?" the woman asked, matter-of-fact.

"Stuart C. Bissette."

Silence.

More ear pounding.

"And you are?"

"Jan Reardon…Mr. Bissette's assistant, here at Finneman and Blakeslee." My cell, paid for by my dad, has a New York City number; it could work. Still, the deal, so seemingly straightforward, was already torquing badly. I never tell lies, one, because I don't think I can pull them off, and two, because I think lies disrupt the order of things. I'd been beaming false data via text message to my mom all afternoon, but that was different.

My scalp prickled and the pounding in my ears was so intense I couldn't hear what she was saying. I plowed on, "I believe Mr. Bissette had originally booked the suite for the week, but…"

"No, just Saturday to Sunday."

This threw me. "Uh, uh, umm…"

"But don't worry. The same arrangement, the suite, is available."

The suite. I didn't know what I thought I'd be getting. I wanted to ask how much a night, but I didn't dare.

I considered hanging up. She didn't know me, she couldn't see me, but I had given her the number, and my dad's name, and the name of his secretary, and the name of where he worked. She'd probably think we got disconnected and call back. The suite then.

Kal hadn't come back. I had walked over to Union Station, thinking I'd find him waiting for a train back to Ohio. I had to give him his letter. And tell him I believed him.

When I got there, I felt stupid; his train would be long gone. I should have followed him right away, caught up with him and apologized, but instead I had just stood there like an idiot trying to bend time.

After that, I had to keep moving.

I'd left my suitcase at the giant front door of the Archives. I thought I'd go back for it, but I didn't. I walked to Georgetown. It's far but I wanted it to be far; motion is breathing. Air in, air out, air in, air out, all the way to Georgetown.

Shopping happened. New stuff. What else could I do? My suitcase was official fallout. I was anxious about that and about my mom. If she knew I had skipped out on the elite experience she imagined me having, her head would vaporize. I paid for the clothes and a new duffel bag with the same credit card I had used to rebook the hotel room. Swiping the card and signing my dad's name was fair—he owed me—and unfair. It was upsetting, and reminded me of the original paradox—have it but don't use it.

None of it was my fault. Feeling the sureness of that truth made me feel better. So much better, in fact, I considered re-signing myself up for camp, but I didn't. It was too late.

Anyway, what if the kids there thought my fractal was stupid? I'm a crap-to-average student. Maybe I don't belong there.

I had used my fractal to get out of going to Dr. Langold. My mom's crazy afraid of our present setup—her, the new husband, the hatchling, and me—becoming a dysfunctional family. Me in therapy is a noble thing because it's really her in therapy. This is one of the few things I told Dr. Langold that didn't involve advanced mathematics. She didn't say a word. Mom writes the checks, right?

I'd catch the bus from school and lie on her comfy sofa for an hour. You could sit in a regular chair or on the shrink couch as if you were talking to Dr. Freud himself. I chose the couch, partly because it made Langold happy and partly because I wanted my mom to get her money's worth. But that's all I did for either of them.

Mostly I recited equations. "Dr. Langold," I'd say, "if you want to comprehend me, you need to understand my problems." This is how I kept her from vacuuming my brain on account of Mom's need. When she began writing them down, I got nervous like maybe I was revealing too much. I considered throwing her off the trail with some bad math, but I couldn't bring myself to do it.

If she solved any of my problems, I never knew about it. My mom needed me to go; I went. It relieved her worry about us all becoming dysfunctional—and, after six sessions, I got a pair of boots from Neiman Marcus.

We were standing on Wisconsin Avenue, my new boots resting safely in their gigantic bag, when I told her I had entered the National Elite Science, Technology, Engineering, and Math Competition and wouldn't have time for Langold anymore. College application decoration. She said okay.

Her job on me is done when I get into a Top-Tier University. That's where she and my dad met, at a Top-Tier University. I guess they learned a lot of useful stuff because they both have Good Jobs. They don't speak except through lawyers, so they did miss out on some kind of lesson, don't you think?

I stare up at the hotel ceiling trying to figure out what I'm doing here. The ceiling is gorgeous—old-fashioned and intricate. I look at the drapes. I spy something toile. I miss Avilov. My mom pays me a stupid amount of money to walk him, so it ends up being him and me a lot of the time. He doesn't know it's a paid arrangement and likes me best anyway. He lives in my room and kept me company all those hours I worked on my fractal.

So yeah, Avilov is named after the Caps' Avilov. My mom loves hockey. When the real Avi scores, it's like the people in this city get hopeful for a minute—like they believe maybe one person can make difference after all, that everything's going to be all right. I've seen it with my own eyes, though I still don't know if my mom named our dog Avi because she believes or she doesn't believe.

Thing is, Avilov isn't a congressman, or a high-stakes lawyer, or a think tank brain, he's just a kid out of Russia. But he's a kid doing the thing they don't let kids do anymore, *his own thing*. I guess I'm doing that now, *my own thing*. It doesn't feel too good.

I wish Kal hadn't walked away from me. I wish I hadn't said that about his grandfather. I want to know what happened to Mike Kovac, but Kal doesn't have a choice, like he was assigned the task of searching for him at birth.

I plump up the pillows and sink in to read the *Post*, leisurely and in order. When I finish Section A, I put it back together, fold it, and pick up Section B, the Metro section. Then I stuff a pillow in my mouth so no one can hear me scream bloody murder.

Under the headline "Terror Threat at the National Archives," there's a picture of me. You can't tell it's me, but it is. I'm standing near a giant pillar and next to me is my suitcase. My backpack's over one shoulder and you can see the North Face logo on my jacket and my long ponytail.

Couldn't a homeless person just have stolen that stupid suitcase and enjoyed a new wardrobe? That's what I figured would happen when I knew I wasn't going back for it.

I tell myself I have nothing to worry about, I didn't do anything wrong, plus my mom's a lawyer, plus I *have* a lawyer. I also know I won't be calling my mom on vacation, my force field is twenty texts strong, there's no undoing it.

Yeah, I have a lawyer, Maria Sincavage. When I was little I couldn't say her name, so I called her Cabbage and I still do. My mom and dad only communicate through her. I could pull off some crazy stuff, but Cabbage is always cool about things and one whiff of a dysfunctional transaction and she'd be in hot water with one or both of them. I've been with Cabbage a long time and I'd like it if she stuck around.

I want to call Cabbage, but she's not that kind of lawyer. I suppose she'd know what to do, but what if her picture got in the paper? Her escorting me down the courthouse steps through a mob of cameras and reporters? My mom has had side shots of her face in those pictures lots of times. She doesn't mind a bit, but Cabbage would. I couldn't risk her getting mad at me; she's never been mad at me in my whole life.

I put the paper to the side and watch a movie about a blind girl who saves her mother after she passes out drunk and falls into their swimming pool. Later you see the reason she's blind is her mom drank a fifth of bourbon every day of her pregnancy or something like that. The girl finds out and goes crazy breaking all the glass in the house and in the end her mother gives up her drunken ways and they hug and ride a horse together.

After the movie, I get out of bed and walk around the suite looking at things. The furniture makes you feel like George Washington's still in town, all very stately and polished. There's a fireplace with small plaster faces across the trim. They're not friendly.

I open the mini bar and eat a can of cashews. I consider opening a beer or a small bottle of Scotch. I've sat with my dad tons of times while he orders one or the other. I unscrew the cap of a mini bottle of Johnnie Walker Black and touch it to my tongue. It burns a hole in it and clears my sinuses. I don't want to be so messed up on Scotch I can't figure out what to do about my shadowy picture being on the cover of the Metro section or start any habits that would blind the daughter I might someday have. I screw the cap back on and put it back.

I get dressed in my new jeans and the Clash T-shirt I found at a vintage shop yesterday in Georgetown. My dad would love seeing me in this T-shirt. Too bad for him. I walk a few blocks to the drugstore, having decided to solve my problems one step at a time.

Back home—hotel home not home home—in the bathroom, I cut my hair short with a pair of scissors I just bought. It's a pretty good job. Am I crazy? Only yesterday I wouldn't have cut my own hair if you paid me a million dollars. Today it seems like the only sensible thing to do. I dye it Sunlight Blonde. It should be called Harsh Sunlight. It's not the golden sunlight streaming through an upstairs window I had envisioned. It's—harsh. No one's gonna be handing over an expensive camera anytime soon, so there's that.

I like it fine, but find myself again wishing that I hadn't doubted Kal's story. My new hair makes me feel like I'm about to start something, but it's no good alone.

When I am sufficiently changed, I pick up the Metro section:

Terror Threat at the National Archives

An unidentified woman caught here on security camera abandoned a suitcase at the top of the steps leading to the portico of the National Archives building where the Constitution, Declaration of Independence and other documents precious to the United States are kept. The building remained on lockdown for five hours while it was searched. The suspicious suitcase was confiscated by D.C. and Virginia bomb squad units. Inspection of the bag showed it to be harmless.

The bomb squad? I guess I might be in trouble, but for what? What if I had hurt my arm and couldn't drag my suitcase anymore? I would have had to leave it. I never expected to see my suitcase again, but looking at its picture in the *Post*, I wish I had it. Having it was the person I was yesterday, and not having it is the person I am today, and for all my shopping, I hadn't thought to buy underwear.

I'm tired of being mad at my dad, but it's his fault. Why was my suitcase left at the National Archives? Because he screwed up our week.

Besides, I'm not even in trouble; everyone now knows my suitcase isn't dangerous. I had cut and dyed my hair for nothing, but between that and not wearing any underwear, I feel like I might be guilty of something, just not trying to blow up the Declaration of Independence.

I go over the window and look down. There's a parade on H Street, lots of people carrying giant silvery pink cherry blossom-shaped balloons assumedly in honor of our friendship with Japan, surely some kind of Plan B since the actual ones haven't arrived.

Long Tieng is Lima Site 20A, or Lima 20 Alternate, or just Alternate. It's the busiest airport in the world, with more planes coming in and out of here than Chicago O'Hare. It's a big, busy, invisible spook city. I need to get to know some of these CIA men better, ask how they do it—exist and not exist. But they're not much in the habit of explaining themselves.

The Ravens seem mostly to come up from Saigon, handpicked out of the Air Force. Working 01s and Bird Dogs on Forward Air Control. They fly low and slow, looking for and marking targets. No uniform, no military ID, no blood chit, nothing. They go down, they got each other to get out, that's it. The U.S. Government's not coming for a man who's fighting a war that doesn't exist.

I'm still regular Air Force, mostly doing utility. I have my military issue ID, tags, and a blood chit. If I get lost or stranded, it's supposed to be a deal for the guy who finds me. U.S. will give them money if they get me home safe. Blood says we're friends, chit says we'll pay in case friendship's not enough. Maybe it works. Maybe it doesn't.

Air America pilots are here too. Some are familiar from the bars in Vientiane. They're labeled civilian. They aren't. The flying isn't easy for them either. A lot of them been around for years, making rice drops, rescues, deliveries.

CHAPTER SIX

A Girl in a Kimono, Texting

o not disturb my circles. Archimedes said that a couple thousand years ago. They were his last words. He had defended the city of Syracuse with his inventions for years. He burned Roman ships with a giant mirror! When they finally did conquer Syracuse, they wanted him to get up from what he was doing to go and meet the Roman general. He refused. He was working on a math problem in the sand. He was drawing circles; that's when they cut off his head.

These days they'd call it cop suicide, where you do something terrible and run from the cops until they shoot you and you die. If it's true that the angrier you are the more violent the suicide—hanging say, over sleeping pills—cop suicide is up there.

I don't think Archimedes was angry. I think he said it so he wouldn't have to give his smart brain to the Romans. Or maybe he really did just want to finish his thought.

There's a statue of him, out in front, on the top of the entrance to Union Station and everywhere else, inside and out, are statues of Roman soldiers. What idiot put that combination together? A mathematician surrounded by his enemies.

I go back there to look for Kal. I'm overflowing with worry about my picture in the paper and about his letter.

He's not there.

I walk to the Archives. I figure if I'm him looking for me, that's where I'd go, but he's not there either. I don't dare go up to where we sat, where I left my suitcase. Even with short blonde hair I don't want to get caught on the security camera again. Anyway, the door to get inside is down underneath the stairs. There's a long line wrapped around the corner, but I stand in it anyway. It's cold and I'm not wearing my coat. Twice I almost go back to the hotel, but I'm hoping Kal's inside.

I make it in and through security. I go up into the Rotunda, the big room where the Declaration of Independence and all the other stuff is. I stand in the dim light and search the bodies in the crowd for Kal's lean line. I search the faces for his one white eyebrow. The place is jammed. Everyone wants to see freedom for real. Well, not everyone: I'm there looking for Kal, but I wait my turn to look because I don't know what else to do.

It's too faded to read. I don't remember the Declaration of Independence this way. Maybe last time I was here I was too short to see it. Wouldn't someone have lifted me up? I don't know. I look and look, not at the documents but at the people. The whole country is here, the whole world actually. A man with a baby strapped to his chest, a lady in a sari, a couple of old crocodiles in matching track jackets, all kinds of packs of kids, a woman dressed in layers of soft pink with a cream-colored hijab trimmed in pearls. No Kal.

I console myself with a replica, readable Declaration of Independence from the gift shop. Even the United States of America has its own merch. I sit down on a marble step, not caring how crowded it is.

"You can't sit here," a guard says.

I'm testing my rights. Strike one.

"You can't sit here," he says again.

"I'm here for a research project," I say, a half lie.

"That's fine, but you can't sit here. The research room is around back."

"Wait, there's more stuff?"

"A lot more. It's closing now. Come back tomorrow."

Walking back to the hotel without a coat, I'm cold as stone, same as the buildings I'm passing. Granite, invisible.

The Hay-Adams lobby is warm with light, but better than that, there's a girl perched on the edge of a velvet chair wearing a kimono. It's orange with blue cranes flying through pink clouds. Everything about her is still except for her thumbs, which are flying, a level of texting even I've never seen. She doesn't see me.

Maybe I'm lonely. Maybe I'm mesmerized by her long, straight, black hair against the vibrant colors of her kimono, or just the whole texting girl in a kimono thing. I walk over to her, half bend at the waist and give a little wave.

She looks up and smiles, not a polite smile, but a whole face smile. She's glad to see me. Her thumbs finish what they're saying.

I'm no longer made of granite, cold and invisible, but of silk, multicolored and fine, and suddenly—conspicuous. I hurry to the elevator. I don't look at anyone. I don't want anyone looking at me or asking about my dad. I go upstairs and order room service—a hamburger and French fries and hot cocoa.

No one knows what the Plain of Jars is exactly. It's confusing, big and strange—mostly called PDJ, left over from the French, Plaine des Jarres. It's a hundred miles wide, and sits high in the mountains. The thing that makes it like nothing you've ever seen is that most anywhere you look are huge stone jars at least five feet tall, some by themselves, some gathered around each other. They're everywhere up there. Hmong say there's a giant sleeping nearby, the jars are where he keeps his rice wine. I think it's an ancient burial ground. No one's ever found bones in them, but it's not that kind of burial ground. It's the souls that need safe-keeping.

Hmong have at least three souls each. When they die, one goes to be with the other dead souls in the family, one stays at the burial place, and one's reincarnated back into the living family. I think those jars are for holding souls.

Vang Pao and the Pathet Lao are battling for the PDJ—the bombing doesn't end.

I don't fear flying or for my body but I do fear those sleeping souls on that wide, open plain. If I thought my soul was going to be laid to rest in a big stone jar on a high flat plain as far away from the wars of nations as a man could dream and found in-stead it was in the middle of a secret, deadly game—well, that'd be a bad thing.

CHAPTER SEVEN

The Ravens

ly until you die. There's a red rubber stamp at the top of the page: FOIA. That stands for Freedom of Information Act and it's been on the top of almost page I've looked at since this morning. FOIA is my right to know what the government's been up to. *Fly until you die.* It's the same thing that's written on the inside of Kal's envelope, which I still have.

I take a picture of the page with my phone. I'm allowed to do that. I pack up the pages I've been looking at and walk them over to the return desk. I have to get back to D.C., which means reversing the ten thousand steps it took to see these words.

It started this morning with me signing a form swearing under penalty of law that everything written on it was true. It wasn't true. I put down a made-up name, Renee Mandelbrot, so, yes, I lied on the form that got me into the rooms underneath the Declaration of Independence. Now I'm thinking about lies and freedom, but then I just wanted to get in the door without anyone knowing I was here.

That lasted about five seconds. When I asked the lady hovering at the entrance about the Vietnam War, she said I had to go to College Park, Maryland. I didn't want to go to College Park, Maryland, but she whooshed me out the door saying the shuttle bus was about to leave.

I ran and caught it and then I was in College Park, Maryland, standing in front a boring glass building. Not anything like the main Archives with steps and columns and the biggest door in the world.

Getting inside was another rigmarole, metal detectors, signing in, security, over-curious people hovering around. Every step of the way, I flashed my Renee Mandelbrot ID.

Finally back in D.C., I roll off the shuttle. I'm tired and hungry and have something important to tell Kal, if I ever see him again.

I go to the front of the Archives and sit at the top of the steps where we'd last been together. So what about the security camera. The sky is clear, but it's getting late. The visible light waves are changing from short to long, the nighttime version of the morning show at the Lincoln Memorial. An American flag, high up on a pole out front, flaps wildly. I sit on the steps in the cold evening light and wait for Kal. He must be looking for me.

And he is. He sees me and runs up the steps.

"Please tell me you have my letter," he says, breathing hard.

"Yes, yes, here." I take it out of my backpack and hand it to him. "I'm so, so sorry. I've been looking for you…"

"It's okay, it's okay." His face is relief.

I don't know how to tell him I've spent the whole day working on his problem.

He squints, "Your hair."

"Yeah, different, huh. There was a—a misunderstanding."

"You should have seen the place. There were fire engines and police cars all around the block."

"I left my suitcase."

"It was crazy," Kal says, then pauses. "I was gonna go home. He wasn't on the Wall. I was on my way to the station and I got turned around and I ended up over by the Washington Monument. The sky was full of kites."

"The Kite Festival!"

"So many kites. Everything. All kinds of kites—I couldn't leave. And then I felt bad I left you standing there, I mean, come on, you're the only person I know in Washington, D.C. And then I realized you had my letter and I ran all the way back, but you were gone."

"I have something for you," I say awkwardly, thinking of myself on the steps, waiting so forgotten for so long. "I found *fly until you die*. During the Vietnam War, there was another war, a secret war run by the CIA. It was in Laos, the country to the west. It was a dangerous, secret war that the U.S. government denied for years. *Fly until you die* was a motto—of the pilots."

"I know," he said. "The Ravens."

"Maybe that's what happened, maybe he was a Raven." I thought I had found something new, but I hadn't.

"Thanks for looking."

"I have a present for you." I hadn't bought it for him, but I want to give him something. "It's the Declaration of Independence," I say, taking it out of my backpack where I'd crammed it yesterday. "Use it wisely."

Kal uncrumples and unscrolls it and holds it out ceremoniously, then he lets it flip closed like a window shade. "You know," he says slowly, teacher to student, "it was written by a guy who owned slaves." He pauses, then continues in the fake teacher voice, "It makes all of this," he opens it back up, "so very difficult."

I don't understand any of it anymore either.

We cross the street to the Sculpture Garden and are barely on the curb when two black Suburbans fly by, sirens and red and blue lights blaring and flashing. A black Town Car speeds behind it. It's the girl in the kimono. Her head is hanging out over an open window, and the wind is whipping her long black hair.

We go into the Sculpture Garden and walk over to the big silver tree. I spy something silver. Kal touches it. "Just like everything else here, made to look real but so obviously not real. A war run by the CIA, is that even possible?" he says.

My phone buzzes. It's a text from my mom. I'm startled. She hasn't been bugging me, just responding to the texts I'm sending, which are a lot. Offensive defense.

Did you find the surprise in the inside pocket of your suitcase? Everyone's favorite little blue box!! Miss you! Love you!

I text back, LOVE IT! Miss you too.

Oh no, when my mom's feeling guilty her presents can be extravagant. Little blue box means Tiffany. If I show up at home without whatever is in my suitcase plus not having gone to STEM camp, she'll spit blood.

"Did you see what they did with my suitcase?" I say to Kal.

He shakes his head.

"I have to find it." And I do, it's nonnegotiable. "Will you help me? Please?" My wanting to help him is coming out backwards, but I need my suitcase.

Landing in Vientiane is easy compared to the dirt strips every-where else in Laos. Had lunch at the Embassy. The attaché to the ambassador was there. Also, an Air Force colonel, one of the princes (really!), a guy from Long Tieng I had transported—CIA probably, couple of others. There was a gal there too, another American, Peggy; she looked way too young to be so far from home.

I asked what she was doing in Vientiane and she said, "Same as you." Asked if that meant she was flying planes and she told me no, she was a nurse.

It was strange to be in my white dress uniform, enjoying a lei-surely lunch and French wine when I had so recently been drop-ping bombs on the PDJ.

There is a massive monument going up in Vientiane decked out with Buddhas and Naga snake gods and half-woman half-bird kinnari. When I brought it up, there was pindrop silence. Like the dinner we told your parents about the baby and that I had signed on for flight school and was coming over here.

CHAPTER EIGHT

Evasive Authority Interaction

ring the bell at the fire station. No one answers. It's the closest one to the Archives. They have to know something. I ring again. Finally, a man, so big he takes up the whole frame, opens the door. I've woken him up.

"YES?" he booms. I had planned on getting snippy about getting my suitcase back, but it's out of the question.

I stick out my hand, introduce myself, and ask him about my suitcase in one breath. He steps back, looks at me, and laughs. It's a laugh as big as he is.

My face is a frozen smile.

"Sergeant Frank," he shakes my hand, pumping it up and down cheerfully, and then shakes Kal's the same way.

"You, little lady, caused quite a commotion."

I should be annoyed, no one calls me little lady, but there isn't room with this guy.

"I didn't mean to leave my bag, it was a-a-an emergency." I side glance at Kal to see what he thinks about my calling his running away from me an emergency. Nothing.

"Oh you can say that again. You were in the paper. Did you see it?" He tilts his head, "Was that you?"

"I changed my hair."

"I see." He laughs again, big and loud. I should be insulted but, really, there isn't room for it.

I say as much as I can without revealing that in some circles, I'm classified as missing. He doesn't have my suitcase but he's pretty sure he knows where it is. We go into his office where he starts making phone calls. He booms hellos and greetings, asks about somebody's kid's baseball game, all the while chuckling and smiling while Kal and I sit across from him trying to look as law abiding as possible.

"Um hm, uh, huh, yes, I know. Yes, right here," he says into the phone and then to me, "Okay, we got it, they're waiting for you at the police station."

I don't want to meet any more cops. This guy's okay, in fact, he's awesome, but he's not a cop, he's a fire guy. Sergeant Frank walks us to the door and I thank him in a low voice. I'm nervous. Things are getting out of hand.

He smiles, shakes his head, and says, "It's all right; you're all right."

I hug him. It just comes over me. Not a prissy girlfriend hug but a good tight firehouse hug, and for a minute I think things might, against all present evidence, be all right.

NINETY-NINE TIMES OUT OF A hundred I wouldn't choose to be face to face with a police precinct captain. But this time I have to go through with it and here I am. Kal came with me, but he wouldn't come in. Who could blame him?

I had thought about telling my mom the Tiffany box was stolen from my dorm room, but what if it was a diamond or something? She'd raise holy hell. I'm more afraid of her than going to the police station and turning myself in as a terrorist.

"A lot of resources were utilized to determine your suitcase was harmless." This guy isn't too scary, but he's dead serious. His name tag says Captain Dean Willingham. He doesn't bother introducing himself as he leads me to his office, points to a chair in front of his desk where I'm to sit, and sits down facing me.

I apologize. I apologize again.

He's going to give me my suitcase; I need to get through this. I didn't do anything wrong on purpose, but that doesn't matter to him: there had been trouble and resources were utilized.

He stares at something behind me, not saying anything.

I had already apologized twice. Can't that be enough? As I sit here waiting for him to give me my suitcase, something catches up with me. I really *am* sorry. I'm sorry to be here. I'm sorry I won't be showing everyone at STEM camp my fractal. The only thing I'm not sorry about is finding out about *fly until you die.* I'm not sorry about that.

Captain Willingham asks if I have any ID, and I show him my DC One Card. All D.C. schoolkids have them so we can ride the bus for free. For a short second I think about skating through this encounter as Renee Mandelbrot with my freshly minted Archives ID, but I don't. He looks at the one I gave him and looks at me. Satisfied that my face matches the photo, he puts it on the desk between us.

"Are you running away?" he says.

My eyes brim with tears, but I hold onto them. I look down and one falls out against my will, making a splotch on my jeans. When I can trust my voice, I look up and say, "No."

He leans back in his chair, lays one arm across his chest, rests the bent elbow of the other on it, and rests his chin in his hand.

"My mom's out of town, on vacation, I'm staying with my dad who's visiting…at the Hay-Adams. I was on my way there and got sidetracked," I say, picking up confidence as I go along. It's practically true. I show him the keycard to my room at the Hay-Adams. "He's in meetings all day, or he would've come." I want the Hay-Adams to purchase my escape. I figure if I'd shown him the key to some lousy hotel he'd be on the phone to Protective Services in two seconds.

His silence tells me he won't be bought; he doesn't care what kind of hotel I'm staying at.

I dig Cabbage's card out of my backpack and put it on the desk next to my One Pass and hotel keycard. "My lawyer, if that helps." I know how it sounds, but that's the deal, that's me.

Captain Willingham shifts in his chair, leans forward, and puts his elbows on the desk. He stares at my credentials.

"Can I call her? I get a phone call, right?" I try to say it jokingly.

"Yes, you should call her."

"Here?"

"Yes, here."

Cabbage picks up right away. This doesn't always happen. I'm really, really glad to hear her voice. I say I lost a bag, I'm at the police station, could she help me out. She asks to speak to someone there, and I hand the phone over.

When they finish talking, Captain Willingham gives me my phone and says, "She's going to fill out a lost property report

online. When that comes through, you can sign for your bag."
He gets up and leaves.

I wait a long time, an eternity. His office is filled with plaques
and citations and framed documents. There's a small MIA POW
flag pinned up behind his desk. It's the same one they have at the
Wall, black, with a picture in white of a bowed head in front of a
prison. It says, *You Are Not Forgotten.*

When he returns, he puts a form on the desk and hands
me a pen.

"I have to read it," I say.

He motions for me to be his guest. I skim it. My mom would
hate to see me not reading it word for word, but I can't focus. I
want my bag and to get out of here.

I sign and hand him the form.

He looks at me.

I want to tell him a truth. Mine isn't available so I borrow
Kal's. I say we're trying to find someone who didn't come home
from the Vietnam War. I tell him about fly until you die, and the
secret war in Laos. I hope Kal doesn't mind.

Captain Willingham doesn't relax his serious face. He listens.
When I finish, he asks me if I'd like to take a short ride.

The royal family took the money the United States gave them to improve the airport in Vientiane and built that big monument instead. I ran into Peggy in the hotel bar. She told me they call it the Vertical Runway and in no circumstances is it discussed at an Embassy luncheon.

We stayed awhile shooting the breeze. Either life at the Embassy is fairly placid or she wasn't letting on what she was up to. Given my own secrets, I wouldn't begin to guess what she was or was not up to.

CHAPTER NINE

Arlington Cemetery Is a Fractal

Kal is sitting on a stone wall in front of the station. Behind him is a row of bare Yoshino trees. Even the police station would get their cherry blossoms eventually. His hands are shoved deep in his puffy orange jacket.

As Captain Willingham and I walk by, I say, "C'mon," casually as if I'm not walking over to get inside a police car.

Kal comes on, but bugs his eyes at me behind Captain Willingham's back.

"Wait, what about my bag?" I stop.

"You can get it after."

So we're riding in a police car, the very last place I ever expected to be, though I recommend it. It's fun once you let yourself believe you're not in trouble.

We pass the Watergate, the Kennedy Center, the back of Lincoln. We cross over the Memorial Bridge, heading toward Virginia. I spy something silver. It's still far away, but I can see three silver arcs.

I point it out to Kal. "Air Force Memorial."

"For who?" he says.

I think it counts for Mike Kovac, but I don't want to argue if he doesn't see it that way. Below us the Potomac River is rough and dark.

"Where are we going?" Kal mouths the words.

I shrug. Maybe Reagan Airport to be smuggled out of the country and trafficked as human slaves.

We roll up to Arlington Cemetery and park right out front in the no parking area.

Is he taking us to the Tomb of the Unknowns? I hope not. I don't think that will be enough for Kal. I ask if that's where we're going and he says, "The soldier from Vietnam isn't there anymore. There's a soldier from World War I, World War II, and the Korean War. The soldier from Vietnam was identified so they moved him to his own grave."

"Oh." I say, absorbing this fun fact. Well, fact.

Is Mike Kovac buried here? Is that good or bad news? I'm scared Kal is getting mad at me again. He didn't sign on for a trip to Arlington Cemetery. He keeps shooting me looks.

We walk up Grant Drive to a small monument. It's a square stone on the ground right off the road with a brass plaque on top.

DEDICATED TO

THE U.S. SECRET ARMY

IN THE KINGDOM OF LAOS

1961 – 1973

IN MEMORY OF THE HMONG/MONG AND LAO COMBAT VETERANS
AND THEIR AMERICAN ADVISORS WHO SERVED FREEDOM'S
CAUSES IN SOUTHEAST ASIA. THEIR PATRIOTIC VALOR AND
LOYALTY IN THE DEFENSE OF LIBERTY AND DEMOCRACY WILL
NEVER BE FORGOTTEN.

YOV TSHUA TXOG NEJ MUS IB TXHIS

LAO VETERANS OF AMERICA

MAY 15, 1997

"The date you see on this stone is the day the government
revealed this war," Captain Willingham says after we've had a
chance to read it. "The Ravens were pilots in Laos. If you find a
Raven, you might find someone that knew your granddad." He
is standing very straight.

Kal steps up on the curb to get a closer look. Captain Willingham moves back and motions for me to do the same. We take
a few more steps backward, then turn around and stare out at the
long sloping hillside, at the rows and rows of gravestones.

"It makes you wonder," he says. It's the first personal thing
he's said since we met.

The graves go on forever.

For every grave there's a person gone, a missing piece in the
life of someone else. I think about my own missing piece. My
cousin Chloe and I spent all our summers together. We're twins,
with our matching eyes and long brown hair, but she's gone, moved
to Paris with her mom, leaving my uncle, me, my grandmother,
all of us, behind.

On the last day we were together we were floating on the sky,
which was a reflection on the lake of a perfect summer day. Chloe
was making me laugh and I was explaining the speed of light in

air, water, and glass. Adults are always telling kids not to blame themselves when someone leaves, but when it's you, you think if you had just been a little more something, they would have stayed.

But none of that, not even the hard, painful hole of their leaving, comes close to looking at these graves. I lose my breath with the realization that I'll see my cousin again; this year of missing her is momentary—but these graves are final and infinitely more difficult.

As sad as this place is, the fractal geometry of it makes me feel better. I should read the names, but I don't want to. I don't want to destroy the fractal. I need the pattern. I look back at Kal and he's on his knees in front of the little monument, pressing his palms into the words on it. His arms are shaking.

"Can I meet you back at the car?" I say to Captain Willingham.

I walk, I breathe. I look out at the elegant geometry of Arlington Cemetery.

There's a sharp bark.

"Oh hey, I'm really sorry. I wasn't watching were I was going," I say, first to the yellow Lab in front of me, then to its owner. The Lab barks again, saying hold it right there.

The owner, a woman, is dressed hat to boots in desert camouflage, like Kal's pants when he was sleeping at the Wall. The dog has a vest in the same camouflage pattern with an embroidered black patch that says Service Dog.

"May I pet your dog?" I say, suddenly missing Avi. "What's her name?"

"Thetis."

I bend down to pet Thetis.

"Please don't."

"Oh, okay, I thought… I'm away from home this week and, well, my dog Avilov…"

"Avilov like Ilya Avilov?"

"Yeah. That's who he's named after, Ilya Avilov. It's the one thing my mom and I could ever agree on."

She smiles a little and lets herself look at me. So if she's not blind, what's with the dog?

"She wakes me up from bad dreams," she says to my silent question, then walks away.

AT THE POLICE STATION, CAPTAIN Willingham wheels out my suitcase. I unzip it and everything inside is soaking wet. Something wells up in me to pitch a fit. I open my mouth to start, but Captain Willingham's face says, *Don't even think about it.*

Without saying anything, he's reminding me of the mass of fire trucks and emergency vehicles that had flooded the scene and that it was somehow my responsibility. Kal moves to take my suitcase in a way that says he agrees that a bag of wet clothing isn't a big deal, comparatively.

"I know someone who might be able to help you further," Captain Willingham says to Kal. "Where can you be reached?"

Kal drills his eyes at me. He wants me to answer. Where is he staying anyway? I decide to be a sport and help. "The Hay-Adams hotel," I say. "Remember?" I keep my voice just inside of snotty. I'm doing some undeserved heavy lifting here, covering for Kal's whereabouts, but okay.

"Yes, of course." His eyes smile. Another first. "You meet Clover yet?"

"No. Who's Clover?"

"Hmmm, maybe you will," he says.

Kal and I get a cab. I lean my head against the window. The evenings are getting lighter but everything is still raw. I feel like an empty paper cup. I had tried to help out about Kal's grandfather, but I don't have anything else to offer him.

I consider my intentions. I don't know what they are. My mom's lectures on decision making, cause and effect, ring through my head. My actions control outcomes, but it isn't working that way. Outcomes are controlling me.

We sit in traffic. I wonder what's in the little blue box in my suitcase. I never told Kal that's why I had to get my suitcase back. He already takes me for a spoiled brat. I don't have the nerve to tell him about the present.

"Where have you been staying?" I say.

He shrugs.

"Who's Clover?" he says.

I shrug.

Still in Vientiane, waiting for orders, sleeping, reading. Went down to the bar and played a game they have here with black and white stones on a hand-carved wooden board. It's easy to learn but has endless possibilities for complicated strategies. I started showing up regularly and became a sort of student to one of the locals, a gentle fellow as old as the mountains, but impossible to beat. When I finally got my orders, I went down to say goodbye and he gave me the board he had taught me on.

CHAPTER TEN

Tomoko

T ext me," I say when we get out of the cab. We had just
been to Arlington Cemetery and all I can think to say is
something you read on a candy heart. He waves goodbye
and floats away.

In the hotel, I practice my I'm Invisible But In Case You Do
See Me I Belong walk. So far, no one's asked any questions about
my dad. The place is like a Swiss bank account, very discreet. It's
funny, when you hang around places that cost a lot of money, you
automatically get treated a certain way. I felt like a black hole sitting in the back of a cruddy cab, but a supernova walking through
the lobby of a fancy hotel. Aren't I the same person either way?

I open up my suitcase as soon as I get to the room. Everything
smells disgusting. I roll it to the bathroom and dump the molding

clothes in the tub. It's a crime scene. I consider sending it all to the hotel laundry, but I've been doing a good job keeping a low profile. I don't want to be caught out by dumping a suitcase full of noxious clothes.

I find the blue Tiffany box in an inside pocket. It's saturated and crushed. I untie the soggy ribbon and take out a cloth pouch in the same pretty blue, with Tiffany & Co. printed on it in black. This is soggy too, but inside, in perfect condition, is a sterling silver Tiffany key necklace. I put it on and go to bed.

In the morning, I order up more Frosted Flakes and hot cocoa. I take a picture of myself wearing the Tiffany key but leave most of my head out of it, so you won't see my hair. I write, Thanks again, Mom. I really love it.

Is that a new blouse? She answers instantaneously.

From Dad, I shoot back and then write that I love her and don't want to be late. Feeling shaky I walk over to the window, open the drapes, and look out over Lafayette Square. Good Morning Mr. President, any secret wars today? I text Kal to meet me there later, but he doesn't answer.

Downstairs, the girl in the kimono is still texting but without the kimono. Today she's on Chanel overload. It looks okay—pretty, actually—just not like anything any girl I know would wear. There's a humongous Chanel bag at her feet, two huge inter-locking C's, in case we're not sure. It's half the size of her whole body. My grandmother has a closet full of Chanel suits but hers are old-fashioned and pale pink or black. This girl's is edgy and the color of a clementine. My grandmother says she's going to leave her suits to Chloe and me in her will. I wish I had one now: I could pass for eighteen, easy.

I sit down in the chair next to her. She doesn't notice. The way her thumbs are flying, she could win a contest. I feel light and fearless. Once you've been accused of trying to blow up the

Declaration of Independence, you start believing you're capable of anything.

I ignore the voice in my head that's my mom's telling me to get where I'm supposed to be. I don't know where that is at this point. I picture her in dive gear, fifty feet down in the ocean, surrounded by brightly colored coral and exotic fish. She's enjoying herself for a change. And me? I'm unrecognizable.

"What, no Hello Kitty backpack?" I say.

She laughs. Her face is as open and happy to see me as it was the other day. She puts her phone on her lap.

"No, that is not my city style." She says each word carefully.

"I guess not." I smile.

She smiles back and that's it, we're out of things to talk about.

I finger my new Tiffany key necklace trying to think of something friendly to say.

She pulls the silver chain around her neck out from under her jacket to show me that she's wearing a Tiffany key necklace too. They're a little different. My key has a swirly flower shape on the end of it; hers has a heart that says, "Please Return to Tiffany & Co."

"They ignoring you at home too?" I say, still smiling, so she knows I'm only kidding around.

She frowns and then brightens and says, "Ahh, black humor."

"Um, so, yeah, you could call it that."

We have matching necklaces. What does that mean, if anything? I was feeling completely free from my mom and here she is again, somehow *involved*.

I tell her my name and she stands up and says, "Tomoko Tachibana." She bows. I stand up and bow too. I want to think it's proof of my worldliness and cross-cultural sensitivity, but mirroring her movements is reflexive.

"Where are you from?" I say.

"Kyoto has been my home since I was born, but we are moving to Tokyo. When I return it will be to our new apartment, my mother and brother are already there." Her English is formal and nearly perfect. She says apartment "apartament."

"Do you know Clover?" I say. She seems to be enjoying my spicy American manners, so I decide I won't disappoint her and throw out something completely random. And anyway, maybe she does know. I'm starting to notice that answers come from all kinds of unexpected places.

"*Yurei,*" she says to herself. She's trying to figure out how to say it to me.

I wait. Something good is coming.

"Clover Adams was the wife of Henry Adams. She died near here, but this spot is where their house was being built, next door to their friends John and Clara Hay."

"As in, Hay-Adams?"

"Yes, and her...spirit, is here."

Now see, it pays to speak up. Clover Adams was a real person, married to Henry Adams. "Henry Adams, the writer?" I ask. I really don't know who he is.

"Yes, and a descendant of John Adams, signer of the Declaration of Independence."

She looks at me quickly like I might be offended she's telling me my own history. She reaches into her purse and pulls out a couple of books to show me she's cheating and I shouldn't feel my country's inferior because she's full of information about it and she can guess already that I don't know anything about hers except that Hello Kitty is from there.

"So Clover's a ghost," I say.

"Yes, a ghost."

"*Yurei?*"

"*Yurei.*"

Turns out, I was to fly the Prince and the guy I brought from Long Tieng to the Royal Palace up in Luang Prabang. It was a good day for it, no fog over the Mekong River, which I caught up with and followed all the way to Luang Prabang.

Karst is mountains and caves carved out of limestone. It rises up ragged and craggy, along the river and off into the distance. You don't want to mess with it in a plane, but it's beautiful.

The Prince was up front with me and was talkative and friendly. When I left them at the airstrip, he invited me to come up for their annual New Year's trip to see the caves filled with Buddhas. I said I'd try. That's flying in the Kingdom of Laos—the wide snaking Mekong River, jagged karst reaching up to take a man down, Buddha-filled caves, impenetrable jungle, and the never-ending battle on the PDJ. Throw into that a CIA man in the backseat and small talk with a Prince and you get the picture.

CHAPTER ELEVEN

Clover

Tomoko tells me the story of Clover Adams. She speaks slowly, her faint accent coming out in extra vowel sounds here and there and soft L's and R's. Her speech, like her suit and her long sleek black hair and her nearly matching Tiffany key, is breathtaking.

Every one loves Clover. She's the wife of Henry Adams. He's a writer and great-, great-something son of some presidents, John Adams—know him from Declaration of Independence fame—John Quincy Adams—don't know anything about him.

Clover and Henry are best friends with John and Clara Hay. They're like a club. Henry writes books and Clover has dinner parties. John Hay had been Abraham Lincoln's assistant; they loved each other like father and son. John Hay could make Lincoln laugh when there was nothing to laugh about, only the crushing pressure of the Civil War. Clara, she's nice too, from a rich family in Cleveland. They're all such good friends they decide to build side-by-side homes on H Street, right across from Lafayette Square, right here where the hotel now stands. Hay. Adams. The Hay-Adams hotel. Here I am.

Besides throwing killer parties and charming the dickens out of everyone she meets, Clover's good at photography. She has her own darkroom. She knows how to develop film and print photographs. She keeps charts and records of work with precise details—exposure times, chemicals, everything. She's talented and skilled and her friends want her to publish her work but her husband won't let her.

Also, Henry, he's got a bit of a thing with the neighbor, Lizzie Cameron—who knows what, love letters for sure—also Clover's dad dies. That cinches it and Clover drinks potassium cyanide, a photography chemical, and kills herself. They find her in her bedroom, dead on the floor in front of the fire.

Henry Adams destroys nearly every letter she'd ever written and just about every single one of her photographs. He destroys all evidence she existed and never speaks her name again. He writes a book about himself and doesn't mention Clover, ever, not one time. Henry and the book are famous. Clover is just gone.

"Did you come here to meet her?" I ask when Tomoko finishes telling me the story.

"No, this is a good hotel for a traveling dignitary, nearby to the White House. We were invited guests there."

I figured. I had seen the kimono, the motorcade.

"My father is the cultural ambassador. He is the one who told me the story of Clover."

"Well, how does he know about her?" How come everyone

in Japan knows about Clover? I try with all my might to get the annoyance out of my voice.

"Clover is the cousin of William Sturgis Bigelow. He is a very important collector of Japanese art," she says. "He was a young boy too when his mother, Clover's aunt, took arsenic to end her life."

Tomoko talks like she's laying railroad track, one word after another. It's mesmerizing.

"Bigelow's collection is in Boston, but from this collection is an exhibit of never-before-shown paintings opening at the National Gallery of Art in honor of the Cherry Blossom Festival here in Washington, D.C. These are the lost paintings of Amayashi. My father had a theory they were here in the U.S. He worked with the Boston Museum of Fine Arts and found them in their storage facilities. We are here for the celebration of her paintings. At the same time, we will enjoy *hanami*."

"And *hanami* is?"

"The custom of viewing cherry blossoms."

"*Hanami* is *late*."

"Yes."

She's not worried at all. I don't get it. What happens if those flowers don't show up? I'm worried for her, and the cherry blossoms, and the city, and me. "Got some Zen in your pocket or something?" I say.

"No." She is expressionless. Either she doesn't have Zen in her pocket or I've insulted her by assuming every Japanese person in the world is a Zen Buddhist.

"I'm sorry. I'm just kidding around." I move my hands back and forth between us: *not sure where the line is; just getting to know you.* I need some international manners, pronto.

"Would you like to know something else about Clover Adams?" says Tomoko more politely than ever. I have offended her and she's rising above it.

"Um, so, yeah," I say, hoping we're back on track.

"Something to see, for you to enjoy. I can show you easily, but first we need a conversation with my father."

I don't want a conversation with her father—the fewer adults in my world right now, the better—but I would enjoy seeing something she could show me easily.

I want to say, "Tell me," but I'm tiptoeing. She's the second most interesting person I've met in forever; she's beautiful, polite, and from out of town.

We find Tomoko's father working at the table in their suite. He's pleased to meet me. He bows and hands me his business card. I bow back.

"I am happy to see Tomoko has met a friend," he says so genuinely, I feel a wave of gratitude.

They have a back and forth in Japanese, and then Tomoko's dad turns to me and says musically, "Okay, see you." I'm glad I didn't try to avoid him.

"I enjoy traveling with my father," says Tomoko when we are going down in the elevator.

"Same." It's true. I love going places with my dad. He's irresistible to me and to everyone. It's taking a lot of energy to stay mad at him.

We're out in front of Lafayette Square, waiting to cross H Street. Tomoko reaches in the pocket of her bright tangerine suit and holds out an empty hand. "Inch time foot gem," she says.

Her almost-perfect English has taken a dive. What is she talking about?

"Not twice this day,

Inch time foot gem.

This day will not come again.

Each minute is worth a priceless gem."

I stare at her and, seriously, I'm sensing an international incident. She shakes her empty hand, like I should take what's *not* there.

"Zen," she says.

"Excuse me?"

"From my pocket."

For the first time since my dad left, I laugh, a real live laugh.

Tomoko laughs too. Her hand bobs in front of her mouth and her head and shoulders shake.

I'm so relieved, I do a little dance across H Street. We pass one of the big statues in Lafayette Square and I shout out the words written on it, "AND FREEDOM SHRIEKED AS KOSCIUSZKO FELL!" and fall wildly to the ground.

Tomoko laughs again. "This way," she says and I follow her into a bricked courtyard in front of a big building off the square.

"Clover," says Tomoko.

She's hiding behind an overgrown rhododendron, but she's there, a statue of a hooded figure sitting on a stone.

"Wait, that's Clover? I know this statue." It's sad and creepy.

"This is a copy of a statue made for her grave," says Tomoko.

"But I haven't been to her grave."

"Yes, the Smithsonian owns a legitimate copy; this one is… unfaithful."

"Pirated?"

"Yes, made without permission." She says it brightly so as not to make me feel bad about any art counterfeiting going on here in the USA.

"The original is in Rock Creek Cemetery, here in the District of Columbia. Henry Adams is there too, but at first it was just Clover."

"And John and Clara?" I say, thinking about the Hays, their side-by-side homes, a.k.a. our hotel.

"No, John and Clara Hay are buried in the Lakeview Cemetery of Cleveland, Ohio. This is also an interesting and famous place."

I for sure never heard of the Lakeview Cemetery of Cleveland, Ohio, but I'm not going to argue. "You know a lot," I say, picturing myself on the losing side of some kind of international Quiz Bowl Challenge.

"Henry Adams drew his instructions for the sculptor from his travels in Japan. He wanted the piece to symbolize the acceptance, intellectually, of the inevitable," she says further proving my point.

"Inch time foot gem?"

"This day will not come again."

I have no idea what we're talking about. I stare at the hooded face of doom. "I don't really think it does, do you?"

"Yes," she said throwing me off. "It does not."

"At least these days a girl can become a famous photographer if she wants, right?"

"That is true. The same here as in Japan."

We walk back into the park.

"Hey!" I shout. It's Kal. He's sitting on a bench staring up at something.

"A blue jay and a robin," he says.

I look up through the bare branches at the birds. They're in some kind of stare-down.

"The robin minds and she doesn't mind," Kal says. "The jay will warn her against squirrels and crows, but if she takes her eye off of him, he'll take her eggs himself."

"Trust issues," I say. "Speaking of, we found Clover. She's a statue…and she's freaky."

"It isn't really Clover," says Tomoko. "It's the way her husband felt after she died."

Kal looks at Tomoko, a little confused, a little amused, and a little awestruck.

I introduce them. Kal puts his hand out and Tomoko puts hers out to shake and also bows. Kal bows back. This bow thing is going viral.

Solo flight back to Long Tieng. It's ten miles up before you can see the curve of the earth, but I fly low and slow. I don't mind. It gives you a different kind of understanding—the rightful place of every small thing.

CHAPTER TWELVE

Kal, Tomi, and Fractal Girl Go to a Show

Tomoko has tickets to see Mata Hari at the 9:30 Club. They're my favorite band. I had begged my mom to see them last time they were here, but she didn't want me going to the 9:30 Club. Kids *are* allowed, I checked. She said the neighborhood is sketchy; the neighborhood's not sketchy.

She took me to see Courtney Collins. That was all fine and well for her and her Facebook page. Her friends wrote stuff like, *Best Mom Ever* and *Lucky Kid*. All through the show she kept asking if I was thrilled. I did my best to be thrilled, but you can't put on a thrill like you put on a coat. A thrill needs to combust internally. Mata Hari at the 9:30 Club? I was thrilled.

Tomoko's dad had not only gotten the tickets, but also gave her the use of his car and driver. Kal was meeting us in front of the hotel, even though we offered to pick him.

I'm contemplating Tomoko on Chanel at the 9:30 Club when she walks into the lobby wearing a leather motorcycle jacket, plaid skirt, black Converse high tops, and dark red lipstick. Her hair's pulled back in a high, tight ponytail.

"Did you get those here?" I ask, secretly complimenting myself on the possibility she might be copying my own gray Cons.

"Made in Japan," she says and bends her foot around to show me that it says so under the ALL STAR on the heel.

Out front, Kal's in black Cons too. He fist bumps Tomoko and says, "Yeah, Tomi." She's so excited about our common footwear and the killer American nickname Kal had just laid on her, she makes us line up our feet side by side and has the doorman take a picture. I believe there's a premium on unselfieable shots. This is one. Off it goes to Kyoto or Tokyo or who knows what worldwide following at the end of her phone.

It's the same doorman my dad was talking to a hundred years ago when I was dropped off here. Has he noticed my dad's not actually here anymore? His face doesn't let on either way. Even if he did, would he rat me out? I think of Clover's grave statue, the acceptance, intellectually, of the inevitable. Well, I'm not dead, so for now, I don't have to accept anything.

I know kids are allowed, but the closer we get to the 9:30 Club, the more I worry that maybe we're supposed to have an adult. I ask to borrow Tomoko's lipstick. She frowns, then brightens and digs around in her purse. She hands me an unused tube of the same dramatic Chanel red she's wearing. I put it on, using the mirror she gives me. Seventeen easy. *Maybe* eighteen.

I hand back the tube, but she says, "No, please."

"Oh no, just to borrow."

She holds up her hand, palm out, and waves it back and forth, "Please, for you to keep."

"No, no, no," I say.

"Hey, Julia, she doesn't want your germs," says Kal.

Tomoko looks at her lap, not having wanted to insult my germs. I look out the window, my germs feeling insulted.

We sit in silence until Kal says, "I hope they play 'No Blind-fold,'" and starts singing, "When the put me in front the firing squad, I said something you might think it was odd, I said, No, no, no, no blindfold, no, no, no, no blindfold..."

Tomoko and I join in— Tomoko, sweetly and in tune; me, as loud as I sing in my room when no one's around. We finish strong, "Noooooooooo blindfold, I AM NOT AFRAID." It's a song about getting shot by a firing squad but I use it for other stuff, stuff that I have to talk myself into doing, like using my dad's credit card when I'm not supposed to and so forth.

Tomoko tells the driver to pick us back up at eleven. This seems tight since Mata Hari won't come on for a while. I, of course, have no curfew, but Kal says he needs to be back earlier.

"Where are you staying anyway?" I ask.

"Ohh, it's kind of a dorm-type place," he says vaguely. It doesn't make sense, but we're pulling up to the club and he jumps out of the car. Tomoko and I scramble out after him.

We get into the club, no parents required. They stamp the back of our hands to make sure we can't order alcohol.

The warm-up band is on. It's not crowded yet, but I want to get a spot up close to the stage. Kal does too, but Tomoko wants to buy us something to drink.

I can't contain myself. I head toward the stage while trying to keep an eye on Tomoko. Kal's halfway between, wanting to follow me but also not wanting to leave her alone.

Two things happen in such rapid succession, you could call it all at once.

First, I look up at the balcony and there, sitting side by side, are Mr. Hammer, my science teacher, and Ms. Wisher, my art teacher. The Hammer and The Wish sitting in the balcony of the 9:30 Club. I'd wonder what the hell they're doing here together, but I can see: kissing.

Second, a huge guy with long wild gray hair is escorting Tomoko from the bar.

I run to them, keeping my head down in case The Hammer and The Wish come up for air. Kal reaches her before me. There's a lot of pointing and yelling between him and the big guy.

The big guy says, "You're out."

Kal stands his ground, but another guy shows up waving his phone. "This is absolutely over. You are welcome to tell your problems to the police, who are on my speed dial."

"What happened, what happened?" My heart is amped as we push through the crowd on the sidewalk.

"Stop shouting," says Kal.

Tomoko's shaking her head saying, "How could I know, how could I know?"

"She tried to order us beers."

We're walking fast, weaving through the crowd.

"What? We have a stamp," I say, showing her the back of my hand.

"Is it a strict rule? I did not know. American rock concert, American beer."

I pat her on the back. "Okay, okay."

I couldn't have stayed anyway, what with not one but two teachers looming. Thank God they didn't see me. It was mega weird seeing them kissing, but thank God they were—thank God for love, or something.

We stop at the end of the block to catch our breath, only to see yet another guy in a 9:30 T-shirt chasing us down. He's even bigger than the other two. He's covered in tattoos with rings through his nose and both eyebrows, and piercings up and down his ears.

We all three jump, but Tat Man gives us the calm down motion. Kal squeezes my arm.

The guy says, "Listen, my buddy's working over at a place on U Street, there's a teen thing going on tonight."

"Mata Hari!" Tomoko says and raises her small fist.

"You blew it, friend," he says gently, "9:30's been in business a long time. Do you really want to be the person that kills the music in Washington, D.C.?"

Tomoko drops her arm in defeat, looks down, and says, "No. Thank you."

"I'll call my friend, let him know you're on your way."

ﷺ

IT'S SOME KIND OF TEEN poetry slam, hard to say what exactly because there's not a lot of people here. Tattoo guy's friend meets us at the door and ushers us over to some very available seating.

A girl is doing a rap thing. I'm too discombobulated to actually listen. It goes on and on. After a while, the rhythm catches my attention. The girl's voice lifts at the end of each phrase and I catch the last words. *SHARP, blah blah blah, HARP, blah, blah blah, APART, blah, POISON DART.* What's she talking about?

She sits down and a woman walks up to the mic and says, "I'm thrilled to see we have a few more participants. We need a total of twenty participants for our funding to be renewed. I think we just made it. Thanks so much for coming!" She holds her hands out to us and claps. The other—what I calculate to be seventeen—kids, clap too.

I elbow Kal. We almost killed the music, now we're on the hook for the poetry. "Do not let this lady lose her poetry money," I say through clenched teeth.

Kal gets up and walks to the mic.

"Any poem?"

"Absolutely. Any original poem."

"Original?"

"Yes, it must be original." She's teetering between ecstatic and crestfallen.

Kal thinks for a bit and then says whatever comes into his head, adding some pauses here and there to make it sound like poetry. A lot of it's about farm machinery. It starts to feel like he'll be at it all night.

After a while, the lady bobs her head up and down and holds out her hands wide to start the clapping, but Kal is on a tear. Finally, finally, he says, "Mass, motion, momentum, this is how things work."

It's a good ending, but all in all a crappy poem. Even so, the idea that he got the ball rolling in saving this lady's poetry program makes it heroic.

I don't know what I'll say. Thankfully, Tomoko volunteers:

A spy, a hand stamp—
my friends and I are refused.
Bye Mata Hari.

A haiku! She's a genius. The scanty audience whoops. The woman clasps her hands under her chin and smiles.

It's my turn. I walk to the front slowly, trying to think of something to say. I stand in front of the mic and wonder at the alternative universe I now inhabit and in what way it connects to my real life. I take a deep breath. "Walt Whitman says, 'For every atom belonging to me as good belongs to you.'" Am I cheating? My grandmother says this when we stand in front of the big painting of Walt Whitman at the Portrait Gallery. I continue.

To be as brilliant as a billion stars,
an old star fuses its own atoms.
It's a violent, exploding, colorful death.
And no even one knows,
not for a hundred lifetimes.
You keep your atoms, I'll keep mine.

I look at the lady. "The end."

I walk to my seat. No one claps. It's not a rambling farm machinery saga or a cogent haiku. Still, I'm Number 20. I saved poetry for the District of Columbia.

Flying with the Ravens again—the best assignment—though I'm still Air Force. Got a regular backseater now, Zaj. He knows the terrain in a way that I couldn't begin to understand.

Went to a party on Vang Pao's roof. He greeted us all personally with a lot of enthusiasm. Drank rice wine and watched the sun set in ribbons of color into the karst. Zaj says everything here holds a soul: a person, a tree, a mountain, a river. I guess we all have our own way of believing. Made me think of the soul of our own hills and river, Suzy. It's tomorrow from where you are. I put a message in these stars so when this night comes over Ohio you'll get it. Still not sending anything through the mail. Soon, again, I hope.

CHAPTER THIRTEEN

Spying Motorized Dragonfly

Good afternoon," I'm humming the Mata Hari Firing Squad song to myself.

"Hello," says the woman at the front desk. She's the one person at the hotel who I sense notices me. I continue to act like a kid whose dad is just back in the room, but I can feel her eyes on me when I walk past.

"Is there a message for Julia Bissette?" I say it sweet and clear, and little loud to hear myself over the song in my head.

She looks at me hard, the robin and the jay.

If you hold still long enough, the other person will fill the empty space until they give their secrets away. My mom practices this on me all the time. It's one of the weapons in her lawyer belt, but she's not above using it on me.

"Yes," she says. She doesn't move.

It's my message, and she's obligated to give it to me. She's the service provider, I'm the recipient. I'll win this face-off, but the arrangement is bought and paid for by my dad—and comes with the bubbling worry about his credit card. I'm a few thousand dollars away from infuriating him. He ditched me, sure, but that will only get me so far.

"May I have it?" I say.

She hands me a letter. *Julia Bissette, Hay-Adams Hotel* is handwritten on the front. The return address is an embossed seal, a white shield with a red multipointed star, the head of an eagle coming out of the top, all in a blue circle. Around the top of the circle it says, *Central Intelligence Agency*, around the bottom it says, *United States of America. HAND DELIVER* is stamped in red.

"Thank you." I think of my short blonde hair and give her a cool smile.

Kal is in the suite. I gave him the keycard and sent him up ahead of me to avoid suspicion, but when I knock on the door he doesn't answer.

Do I even know him? He appears and disappears but never says where he's going. He could be a freak looking for someone to kill on his spring break. Is Kal even his real name? Did he have a grandfather who fought in Vietnam? What is trust? What is safety?

"Clover, what should I do?" I whisper.

He opens the door, "Come in," he says flourishing his arm and grinning. My questions disappear.

I hold up the letter.

"Whoa," he says.

I start to open it, then stop. "Anthrax?"

"I don't think the CIA would put their seal on a secret ops anthrax letter."

I agree and open it. It says,

I'm a friend of Dean Willingham. Would you and Kalman like to come for a tour this afternoon? If so, I'll need social security numbers for both of you. Please call the number on the enclosed card and provide your information. Also, you will need a photo ID to enter.

It's signed *Jim Bennett*. Below his name is the address of the Central Intelligence Agency and some phone numbers.

"Is this for real?" I can't believe it.

"Virginia again," says Kal. "I can't afford a cab out there." His voice is even but his hands are shaking.

"I know." The short cab ride we'd taken yesterday was expensive. I take an Uber to school sometimes but the account tracks to my mom's phone. That was out of the question. "Me neither."

Kal looks around the room.

"I'm using my dad's credit card, the one he gave me for emergencies. He doesn't know it yet." If he thinks I'm a liar and a brat, it's unfair. He has no idea how hard it is to dance between two people who claim it's all about you when it never is.

"Well, what about you?" I say. "Where are you staying?"

"Oh, it's a long story."

I want to know his long story and I want to tell him mine. Thing is, my long story is yesterday's story. I don't know what my story is today.

"I have an idea," I say. I text Tomoko. She'd invited us to see her father's exhibit at the National Gallery and I ask if we can make a stop at the CIA on our way. It's not anywhere near on the way. I write that, right after the part about her getting her father to let her use the car and driver again.

Three and a half excruciating minutes later, she answers, Yes. When?

This afternoon.

Your dad doesn't mind if you use the car without him? I add and hold my breath again.

Yes.

Yes, he minds?

Yes, he does not mind.

I waver. I don't want to kidnap a Japanese diplomat's kid. CIA is not close to National Gallery. I write again.

Yes.

Do you have a social security number?

What is that?

Okay, forget that. Do you have a passport number? Man oh man, I'm thinking on my feet.

Once I have Tomoko's passport number, I call the CIA number on the white card. A voice says hello and I ask if this is Jim Bennett. He says no. I try my mom's I'll Be Silent So You Fill The Space With Information technique. Yes, I try this on the CIA. I don't win. I tell him my name and he freakily says, "Is Kalman with you?" I give him our social security numbers and say we have someone else, someone from Japan. I reel off her name and passport number.

The voice is not okay with this. "Call back in forty-five minutes."

I scrunch my face nervously when I tell Kal what the deal is. He starts pacing around the room, moving his head back and forth, talking to himself.

"I hope I didn't screw this up bringing Tomoko along," I say.

"I hope you didn't either."

WE ARE IN THE CAR nearing the Memorial Bridge when I think I better triple check with Tomoko. "You sure you don't mind this side trip?"

Kal looks at me like, *I thought you said it was okay.* Getting a ride off of Tomoko feels weird. I hadn't told her anything about the Ravens or Vietnam. What if Jim Bennett was going to trust us with something classified but once he saw this Japanese girl—an impeccably dressed and beautiful Japanese girl, but a Japanese girl all the same—he would send us on our way?

Kal says, "We're going to the CIA to find out about my grandfather. He disappeared from the Vietnam War." Then he adds, "You know the CIA? You know what that is?"

"Spies," says Tomoko.

"Yeah. Spies."

"Are you suspicious of me?" She says it so unperturbed I don't know if she knows enough to be worried, doesn't care, or is so bored hanging around the Hay-Adams that she'd go just about anywhere.

Kal says, "No, no, no," with enough tenderness to make my heart zag.

We cross over the Potomac. We're going to Langley; we might as well be going to the moon. I touch my hair and suddenly it hits me. Of all the places to go, the CIA! I lean down so the driver can't hear, and whisper across Tomoko to Kal, "I'm being set up!" How can I be so stupid? I've been insisting none of this Homeland Terror stuff has anything to do with me, but here I am, on my way to the CIA, sent by a cop!

I spend the rest of the ride giving Tomoko the lowdown on my Terror issue, to her dazzled fascination.

There's a sign telling you where to turn to get to the CIA; it's not sneaky at all. Even though I'm petrified, it's disappointing.

Tomoko's driver drops us at the visitors center near the gated entrance, exactly following the instructions we'd been given. My momentary disappointment evaporates at the sight of soldiers on the other side of the gate.

I spy with my little brown eye…two guys with semi-automatic weapons. I spy… my vision goes hyper vivid, making everything over bright and outlined in its own bold color.

Inside the visitors center, we show our IDs. Each of us gets a badge with a big orange V and the words, *Visitor, Escort Required*. We're told to put our phones and wallets in lockers on the wall. We each find a box with a key still in it, lock up our stuff, and pocket the keys. An ordinary-looking guy in a business suit takes us on a shuttle to the main building and through the entrance.

The walls are white marble. The floor is big black and white checks of granite with a huge version of the same seal as on the envelope from Jim Bennett, also in black and white granite. Men and women are dribbling through the lobby, leaving work for the day. Everyone looks as super ordinary as our escort. "Could one of these people be responsible for launching a secret war and denying it for twenty-three years?" I whisper to Kal.

"Shhh," he says, "the walls have ears."

No kidding.

We wait.

A man comes toward us, introduces himself as Jim Bennett and thanks our escort who, I swear, disappears. Or maybe the stress is playing with my mind.

He shakes my and Kal's hand, and turns to Tomoko. She bows, shakes with her right hand, and passes him a business card with her left. She'd been too courteous to hand cards to Kal or me, foreseeing we wouldn't be able to reciprocate. Jim Bennett looks at the card and says something in Japanese. Tomoko answers, also in Japanese. After a few back and forths, Jim Bennett says to Kal and me, "I'm familiar with Tomoko's father."

"So it's okay she's here?" I say.

"Yes, of course," then he turns to Tomoko and asks, "How was your dinner at the White House?"

"Very beautiful and impressive. There were many dignitaries and of course the President," she replies.

Jim Bennett says, "I'm happy to show all of you around. Would you like a tour of our museum? It's not open to the general public." A museum no one's allowed to visit. Perfect.

In the museum, there's a bunch of spy stuff, like a four-pronged spike thing, which lands spike up however you throw it and is sharp enough to puncture a tire. There's a spying motorized dragonfly called an Insectothopter. There's a Letter Removal Device. It's a long skinny pincer that you stick through the small opening in the flap of an envelope; it grabs on to the letter inside and rolls it up so you can pull the letter out without unsealing the envelope. Kal and I exchange looks.

At the end of the tour, Jim Bennett says, "Now for the fun part."

What would a CIA guy think is fun?

"Everyone loves the polygraph test," he says.

It's a trap after all.

Kal's skittish as it is and Tomoko's a visiting dignitary. It's clear I'm to be the designated lab rat, so against my overwhelming suspicions I sit down in the chair. Jim Bennett hooks me up and asks a bunch of obvious questions: What's my name? What school do I go to? Do I like chocolate? That's it. I get out of the chair without incident, but I know that now there's a thin folder with my name on it at the CIA. I don't like it.

We follow Jim Bennett back out to the lobby over to a marble wall with rows of stars carved in it. Above the stars it says, *In Honor of Those Members of the Central Intelligence Agency Who Gave Their Lives in the Service of their Country.* Below the stars, there's a thin book, open and encased in thick glass jutting out from the wall.

"Each of these stars represents an employee of the CIA who died for the United States of America. The stars honor these American heroes and keep their secrets."

"What's the book?" says Kal.

"There's a star in the book for every star on the wall. Some of the identities have been revealed; those names are listed here."

We look at the book. It's chronological, a few stars for some years, none for others; some have names and some don't. Next to 1970, there's a star without a name.

"Nineteen seventy would be about right," says Jim Bennett.

"My grandfather was a pilot for the United States Air Force, he wasn't a spook," Kal says.

If the word "spook" offends Jim Bennett, he doesn't let on. "I understand," he says. "I'm not saying that star is for your grand-father. I'm showing you that men served—men and women—in ways that the public didn't know about. Yes, in secret. And yes, with honor."

I long for the feeling I had watching the long-wave colors of the early light on the steps of the Lincoln Memorial—the feeling I had that our country is the best place on earth.

Zaj couldn't fly. His wife had fetched water from the stream so she'd be ready to wash her baby, which was coming. He told me that when a woman knows she's going to have her baby, she boils a key and then drinks the water to unlock the passage. What key? There were no locks on their doors. Zaj said it's the one made for their wedding ceremony, as a symbol. It's silver, with a spiral on the end. "The spiral is the snail, Mike. In the center, the ancestors; on the outside, the new family." I asked him if he was worried and he said no, the baby would come easily, the key would see to it. I told him my Elizabeth arrived while I was over here. He patted me on the back and said, "Okay, Mike."

CHAPTER FOURTEEN

Secrets

The room is plain carpet, white walls, and imitation wood grain office furniture, either the office of the neatest person in the world or no one. I open a desk drawer. It's empty, so no one.

Jim Bennett asked us to wait here. Will we be interrogated? Tomoko's presence is reassuring. If Kal or I disappear off the face of the earth, that'd be one thing. If Tomoko goes missing, it'd be an international incident.

There's a rectangular gray box on a table being stared at by a man in a large painting on the wall. He's in a dark suit with a stiff pose. There's a limp American flag over his right shoulder. There's no name or date. Maybe he's the 1970 star. Maybe before he got a suit and a stiff pose, he was a Raven. How could someone die for their country and no one know? The Wall of Stars is really, really bothering me. The only American spy I know is Nathan Hale and he's famous. He said, "I only regret that I have but one life to lose for my country." I'd say that. I'd die for my country, I would, but I'd want everyone to know about it.

The box looks like it could be one of a thousand lined up floor to ceiling like books on shelves in some massive warehouse. I imagine the missing tooth of a space where this one goes. Its spine has a metal and plastic cardholder. The card in it says *Vientiane 1969/327*. What could be in the three hundred and twenty-six file boxes before it? How many come after?

Jim Bennett peeks his head in the door and motions for Tomoko and me to come with him. We walk back to the lobby, leaving Kal alone with the man in the painting and the gray box.

He says we can take pictures if we want. My lawyer mom's voice tells me no, but Tomoko is jubilant. Of course we can't take a picture: they took our phones. Another paradox, you can but you can't.

Jim Bennett's a spy. I guess that's how come he can read my mind.

"I'll do it," he says.

Tomoko stands behind the "I" in Intelligence in the giant seal on the floor, and Jim Bennett snaps a few shots with his phone. "I'll send it to you." I have to think a shot of Tomoko at the CIA is a serious gold standard photo op, and I'm glad she has something to show for coming along and giving us a ride.

Jim Bennett tells us the shuttle will be out front in three minutes. We should take it, and he'll send Kal along on the next one.

Fear transmutes my vision again. Three go into the CIA; two come out. Maybe Suzy asked too many questions, and they're taking it out on Kal. I'd just mentally committed to being as brave as Nathan Hale if I had to and what do I do when the time arrives? Board the shuttle bus. I hate myself.

At the visitors center, we get our phones, and right away Tomoko checks hers for the picture on the big CIA seal. It's there and she sets her lightening-speed thumbs in motion.

"Who are you sending it too?"

"My friends in Kyoto. I said goodbye when we came here. When I return it will be to Tokyo. My mother and brother are already in our new apartment."

Right, she'd said that the other day. "How come you're the one that gets to come with your dad?"

"I am interested in his profession. He was at the University in Kyoto for many years, and I often went to see him there. Now he is with the Ministry." Tomoko looks away as she talks. Does being at the CIA make you want to keep secrets? Seems so.

I wait for her to tell me the whole reason. I hate to use this super power on her, but it works.

"My brother does not leave his room," she says.

"Ever?"

"Not so you would know. In Japan, school achievement is very important. We have to get excellent scores on tests so the next school will accept us, and the next one after that, and then to get a good job. A year ago, something happened. My brother decided he did not want to do it. He refused to go school. He refused to leave his room."

I'll be the first to tell you I spend as much time as I can in my room staring up at Cas A, working on my fractals and not talking to anybody. I've imagined every escape hatch possible for my own life but even I hadn't thought to do it *forever*.

"It started when my brother got a bad grade. My mother and father were angry. The next one was worse. They were frightened. And then—he stopped trying."

"What does he do all day?"

"He plays games on his computer and draws, I think."

"How does he go to the bathroom and eat?"

"He comes out to go to the bathroom but that is the only reason. My mother brings his food to the room."

Well, there's the problem. Tomoko's mom and dad were being too nice.

"You do not understand, Julia," she says, though I hadn't said anything. I feel a whir of resentment; of course I get it. "In Japan, the children should be like the parents. When they cannot, sometimes *hikikomori*."

"What's that?"

"*Hikikomori*. That is my brother, when a person won't leave the room."

"You mean it's a *thing*?"

"Yes." Tomoko looks straight at me, challenging me to accept this personal failure in her family—and by the sound of it, her country.

I see her. And I see how many hours it took to speak English so perfectly, how compliant she has to be to make up for her brother's defiance.

Kal appears.

IN THE CAR, TOMOKO GIVES the driver instructions in Japanese. Even though I can't understand what she's saying, I love her for the way she's saying it. She's not condescending the way a lot of kids I know speak to the people who do things for them. And I love her for being here, with us, on our way home from the CIA, not in the lobby of the Hay-Adams, safe and sound.

We're all the way to the river and are crossing back into D.C., when Kal pats his chest and says, "Julia, I'll show you this stuff, but not right this second, okay?"

"What stuff?"

"It's mine."

"Did you steal something from the CIA?" I duck my head low and shout whisper.

"No, the CIA stole something from me," he shout whispers back.

"Are you crazy!"

"Not for taking something that belongs to me; no, I'm not crazy. Anyway, why would that Jim Bennett guy leave me alone with a box of stuff that belongs to me unless he wanted me to have it?"

"I don't know, maybe because he trusted you not to steal it?"

"Trust. Ha."

"What's that supposed to mean?"

"Exactly."

"What are you talking about?" I say.

"Me and the government and trust—none of these things have anything to do with each other. Haven't you been paying attention?"

I stare out at the Potomac. There's a crew shell with eight rowers. I watch their synchronized strokes and wish I didn't have anything to do but match my stroke to the person in front of me.

"I told the driver to take us to the National Gallery if Julia-san and Kal-san would like to view the exhibition," Tomoko says.

Kal and I stare at each other, but when he speaks, his voice is mild. "Julia, would you guys go without me?"

"Ummm." I don't know.

"And this is a big favor—can I hang in your room?" He pats his chest again.

"Sure, yeah sure, Kal," I say and force myself to reach in my pocket and hand him the keycard.

We pull up to the side of H Street between the Hay-Adams

and Lafayette Square. Why, I wonder, looking over at the park, did freedom shriek when Kosciuszko fell?

Kal jumps out of the car like he can't get away fast enough, but before he slams the door, he turns and bows slowly. "Thank you, Tomi," he says. "Thank you very much." He catches my eye and gives me a wave. I want to follow him inside, see what he took from the CIA, but I promised Tomoko I'd go with her. I wave back.

I went to bed late and was sleeping when a shriek ripped through the compound. It jerked me awake, but I didn't hear anything more so I drifted off. The sound came again; it was a woman screaming. I pulled on my pants. Someone was trying to kick the door in.

It was Zaj, holding his wife. Even pregnant, she was tiny. I yelled for him to put her on my bed and ran for Doc.

When I got back, the bed was red with blood and Zaj's wife wasn't moving.

Doc said, "I'm going to help you." He was calm, telling me what to do and where to stand. Zaj stood to the side, murmuring, with his eyes partly closed.

My bag was right there, half-packed for Vientiane, and when Doc asked for clean towels, I didn't have any, so I just started pulling clothes out of my bag and handing them to him. The baby came, bloody and blue. Doc carefully unwrapped the umbilical cord from around its neck and she gave a whelp. I ripped up my white uniform shirt, the last clean thing I had, while Doc washed her and then wrapped her in it.

Doc didn't smile, but he looked satisfied. "A daughter," he said to Zaj, and then to me, "All right then Mike, you just delivered your first baby," which I appreciated since my own Elizabeth came without me.

CHAPTER FIFTEEN

An Artist and an Onna Bugeisha

ere's what I like about Degas's dancers. The expectations are right there out in the open. Like maybe if modern-time parents were more truthful about what's up their sleeves expectations-wise, we could all be a little happier.

Here's what I like about Van Gogh's self-portrait: His face is green because Van Gogh understood light. Also, his eyes match the words in Thomas Jefferson's monument, *I have sworn upon the altar of god eternal hostility against every form of tyranny over the mind of man.*

We're at the National Gallery on our way to see Tomoko's dad's exhibit, but first I had to show her some of the regular stuff. She took shots of me with the Degas dancers, Van Gogh's green face, a zillion things. Somewhere along the line, I'd become fully incorporated into Tomoko's living diary. I actually might be some kind of celebrity in Japan: someday I'll be in Tokyo and people will shout, "It's her, the American girl from Tomoko's Instagram!"

The gallery of Amayashi's paintings is jam-crammed. So many people are here to see this unknown woman's paintings. I'm happy for her, Amayashi, whoever she is.

"This is a compliment to my father," Tomoko says.

She wants me to use the headphones for the listening tour. I never get headphones, I'm allergic to lectures; besides, art is for looking, not listening. She's asking a lot. I consider pretending to listen, but I don't want to offend Tomoko, so I put on the headphones and stand in front of the first painting. I secretly sigh and turn on the recording. "Hey...what!?"

Tomoko laughs.

"It's you!"

"Um, so, yeah."

I think she got that response from me. I'm so proud to be boosting her vocabulary.

"That's so cool!" Now I'm listening.

In Japan, the constellation Orion is Tsuzumi Boshi, a drum with two sides and a narrow middle, or Sode Boshi, the long kimono sleeve of a woman extending her arm to the southern sky. It is also a battlefield from a war a thousand years ago. The big red star, Betelgeuse, is the Heike clan; the bright white star, Rigel, is the Genji clan. The paintings of Amayashi's are a story from that war.

Amayashi was born at night to the sound of spring rain on the cypress bark roof of the small house, away from the palace, where a woman goes to have her baby. Her mother did not scream, for that would have been shameful. Even in the end when the pain was not childbirth, but a woman dying in childbirth, her gasps and tears were as voiceless as the golden Buddha in the Phoenix Temple at Byodo-in.

Harukoshi arrived later, as the soft spring leaves gave the drops of rain they held through the night up to the morning sunshine and the turtledoves murmured, her-her-oo-oo. Harukoshi's mother wept as silently as raindrops disappearing on leaves, as she too gave her body up to the mountain journey of pain, climbing ever higher to join her sister among the stars.

They had been separated for a year, but the twin sisters—still mirror images of each other—had come together to give birth. One had been living with their parents in the palace in Kyoto, while the other had been living a day's travel to the east. It was a year since she'd been swept away by a provincial samurai lord.

I take off the headphones. "Tomoko, did you write this?"

"My father wrote the speech as a combination of the words written on each scroll, his research, and the paintings themselves. I practiced the translation for many hours."

I start it up again.

On their first birthday, the sister cousins' path was strewn with tools of possibility, a writing brush, a painting brush, an abacus, a weapon with a long pole and a curved blade at the end—the naganita. *Amayashi picked up the painting brush while Harukoshi chose the razor-sharp* naganita. *That she picked it up and played with it without injury was confirmation of the correctness of her choice.*

After the ceremony, it was decided that the twin cousins would not be separated but raised together—part of the year at the palace, and part of the year in the province of the samurai.

Amayashi and Harukoshi grew into gifted young women with fine features and long black hair. Their choices were indeed predictive of their futures. Amayashi wielded a brush with ink and color on silk in a manner so lovely, even the Emperor was surprised at her renderings of the Yoshino tree in blossom against the distant mountains. Harukoshi was so skilled at the naganita, *her father knew that she would some day be an* onna bugeisha—*a lady samurai—able to help him defend his estate.*

I flip off the machine again. "Whoa. A lady samurai? What's that about?" I see. In front of me is a painting of Harukoshi and her father riding into battle. She's in full leather armor with a sword at her side and a *naganita* in her hand.

Their fifteenth birthday marked a day leading up to the time when the leisurely and peaceful mannered life of the centuries before would fall away. The balance of power was shifting, and the first great battle between the Heike and the Genji drew near.

Harukoshi watched her last living parent fall into the Uji River, a Heike arrow in his heart. She did not turn and flee, but fought on, wielding her naganita *with precision, the spirit of her just-dead father flaming inside her.*

Shortly before daybreak, she arrived, alive but badly wounded, at the sliding screen of her cousin's palace room. Knowing her own death was near and not wanting any part of her body to be taken for an enemy trophy, she lay in her cousin's arms and begged for protection.

And so, from and for the twin soul of devotion, Amayashi unhinged the long sword from her cousin's belt and swiftly and lovingly severed her head, parting it from the fullest and kindest heart she had ever known.

She wrapped it in the fine silk layers of her own robes, put on the humble clothes of her tutor, and slipped out of the palace through the East Gate.

She traveled the same road the samurai and her aunt had the night he swept her away to his provincial estate. In the morning, she buried the head of her lost cousin in the place on the hillside where she had spent so many hours painting and watching her cousin perfect the art of the naganita. *On it, she planted the small stick of a Yoshino tree.*

I stare a long time at the last painting. I take off the headphones and turn to Tomoko. "How did your... how did your father find these?" I manage to ask.

She is pleased to see I'm overwhelmed. "The samurai's estate remained for seven centuries," she says. "Their children's children each following the path of the one before until the time when the household was sold off and the treasures were passed to the last generation of faithful servants. This is how the scrolls came to be on the shelf of a pawnshop near Kibukawa Station. This is where William Sturgis Bigelow..."

"Clover's cousin!"

"Clover's cousin...found them."

Had William Sturgis Bigelow shown Amayashi's paintings to Clover? I'd have to ask her about it when I got back to the hotel.

"And then your dad found them again?"

"He studied Bigelow's notes and catalogues. He traveled back and forth to Boston many years before he discovered the paintings. And now they are here in honor of your National Cherry Blossom Festival and our friendship."

I don't think of the United States and Japan, but of her and me. I smile and she bows. I bow back.

I walk over to a painting of the cousins looking identical with waterfalls of black hair down to their feet. They're on a porch, playing a board game. There's a snow-covered mountain in the background and blossoming trees near where they lounge. The card beside it says, *Playing Go.*

"I love this one," I say.

"Go is a game we still play in Japan," Tomoko says. "It is simple to learn but very difficult to become a master."

Hmong have each other, the shaman, and the poppy. Someone gets sick: they pinch off a piece from their opium ball, roll it into a smaller ball, and smoke it. If the poppy can't cure it, means it's a soul problem. When a soul's gone angry or missing, people start praying; if praying won't fix things, they call for the shaman and he sets to work getting that soul back.

Beyond the family poppy patch are fields that stretch on forever. They're everywhere now—different from before, when there were fields of rice.

Wrapped sacks of rice have floated down on small parachutes for a long time. The U.S. delivers rice, and the Hmong send their men to fight in return. They all believe—we all believe—in freedom and the great general, Vang Pao. So the tribes grow poppies instead of rice. The general pays the best price, sixty dollars a kilo.

His factory is nearby where he turns opium into Number 4 heroin. If you lay out your palm in the streets of Saigon, a small white packet of Number 4 will appear in it.

I don't speak out against the great General Vang Pao. He is loved on all sides, except of course by the NVA who would give anything for his body to bloody and break. He is a god here. I don't disagree; only a god can understand life and death in the same flower.

CHAPTER SIXTEEN

Blood Chit

It's late when we get back to the hotel. Tomoko and I say goodbye, and for the second time I'm standing outside my door with Kal on the other side wondering what I'll find. He opens the door as soon as I knock, but his hand is in a fist.

"Do you want to see?" he says.

I'm nervous.

He opens his fist and waves out a silk rectangle, walks over to the table, and lays it down.

"It's a blood chit."

He walks over to the window and looks out toward the White House. "Are they all protesting the same thing or different?"

"Different. Blood chit?"

"I don't know how to figure out what matters and what

matters to *me*. Suzy did that: before I was born, she came here to protest. It wasn't the war; it was the river. The Cuyahoga River was on fire. It was so polluted it caught on fire twice. I don't know, maybe she protested the war too, but she only talks about the river. I know there was a time she believed everything the government told her, and then there was a time she didn't believe anything."

Blood chit. The top part is an American flag; the bottom part is the same message over and over in different languages, each of them labeled so you can see what they are: English, Burmese, Thai, Laotian, Chinese, Tagalog, Visayan, French, Dutch. The message is:

> *I am a citizen of the United States of America. I do not speak your language. Misfortune forces me to seek your assistance in obtaining food, shelter and protection. Please take me to someone who will provide for my safety and see that I am returned to my people. My government will reward you.*

"It's so if you get shot down or whatever, the person who finds you will get money if they help you," Kal says.

"How do you know about it?"

He walks over to the sofa and comes back with a book. It's seven or eight inches long and four inches high with a spiral binding. The cover is pebbled leather. It says *Pilot Logbook* in gold letters. I run my hand over the textured surface and hold my breath. Mike Kovac was a pilot in the Vietnam War; maybe in the secret war in Laos. This would have the dates and places he'd flown, tell us where he'd been. I hold it in both hands. Kal gestures for me to go ahead and read it.

It's like the cover says, a pilot's logbook. The pages are pale green with light blue lines and spaces for places, times, and dates, but that's not what's in it. Instead, in the same blue ballpoint pen I'd seen on Suzy's envelope, are long blocks of writing in tight script.

"It's his journal," says Kal.

I sit at the table and read Mike Kovac's words.

The log book got wet from my leaking windshield. I thought of
you every day. We are at war in Laos.

The Plain of Jars, princes, Buddhas, Naga snake gods, a game
with black and white stones, the wide snaking Mekong River, a
CIA man, Ravens, a bed red with blood, Number 4 heroin, Zaj,
a halo of light, the horizon's far margin, the dead.

I read the words, and the words tell me the story. Not all of
it, not everything, but part of it.

Behind the last page are two photographs. The first is a man
crouching down, leaning on his weapon. He's wearing combat
boots, Levis and a white T-shirt, and aviator Ray-Bans. Everything around him is saturated with light and heat. His smile is
on the verge of laughter. I pick up the photo at the edges and
show it to Kal.

"That him?"

"I think so."

I asked even though I knew. The resemblance to Kal is
shocking, except the person in the in the photo looks untrou-
bled and Kal already has a permanent perplexed and worried
crumple to his eyes. That and Kal's one white eyebrow are the
only difference.

The other photo is of two men standing in front of a plane,
same white T's and Ray-Bans, but with rows of bullets criss-
crossing their chests. The one on the left is wearing a cowboy hat.
They also have big, wide, easy smiles. On the back it says, *Mother,*
Skip Travers, Long Tieng, 1969, Fly Until You Die.

"Did you see this?" I said holding up the second photo. "We
can look them up online—well, Skip Travers anyway, try to find
an address or a phone number."

"No," he says, "Let's look on the Wall. We should see first if they're on the Wall."

I don't want them to be on the Wall. They look so young and handsome. I want to jump into the picture and stand next to them. I want to go to a party on Vang Pao's roof and watch the sun set in blazing ribbons over the souls of the mountains of Long Tieng.

"Should we walk over?" I say, even though I don't want to go right now—or ever.

"No," says Kal, changing his mind, "we can look them up."

We do look them up and find Richard "Skip" Travers MIA. I can't put that smiling face and Missing in Action together.

"How about the other one—Mother?" I don't think we can find someone with a nickname, but we try. We search "Mother" on the same site. Nothing.

We have to go to the Wall. We walk through Lafayette Square, past the White House, and over to the Vietnam Wall. It's almost dark and Lincoln is lit up. So is the Washington Monument, a giant white pointy pencil.

At the Wall, we look through the directory and find Skip Travers. We walk all the way down to the middle and up toward the other side, near where I first saw Kal asleep. We find him. Richard Travers, with a plus sign next to his name for MIA. If he's found dead, they'll connect the ends of the plus sign and fill it in to make a diamond; if he's found alive, they'll draw a circle around it.

"Mike Kovac's friend," I say.

Kal touches the name. It's not mine to touch, but I don't think Kal—or Skip for that matter—will mind, so I do.

It *is* my name to touch, and it is possible to lose someone you never met. Now I know.

If Mother and Skip Travers had gone missing at the same time, his name would be near; they're on the Wall in the order of their being lost. We don't know what we're looking for, but we look anyway.

Eventually, Kal takes my hand for us to go. We leave the Wall, but he doesn't let go of my hand. I don't let go either.

We walk all the way to Chinatown, and I would have walked to California if it meant I could keep holding onto his hand.

At the entrance to the Portrait Gallery, I pull his arm and we go up the stairs, inside and down the hall, straight to the picture of Walt Whitman.

The legitimate copy of Clover's statue is upstairs, but I don't want to see it. Walt Whitman had seen the grief of the Civil War in this very building when it was turned into a hospital. He came and read to the wounded and dying soldiers. He wrote letters home for them. I want to know how he went on after that, not how Clover didn't.

OUTSIDE, WE ARE HALFWAY AROUND the block, and Kal says, "Wait, is this where the Caps play?"

The arena where the Washington Capitals play is across the street from the Portrait Gallery—Ilya Avilov and Walt Whitman side by side all season long. If I met Avilov, I'd ask him if he ever took the time to walk across the street to see what's inside. I'd want him to meet Walt Whitman. Walt would love Avi: he'd love seeing that it's still possible to travel to America from a distant land and be wild and free and loved.

"Hey, they're playing the Pens, *right now!*" says Kal. "What were we doing in a museum?"

We can see the game up on the big screen above the entrance to the arena. "I'm sure it's sold out," I say.

"We gotta get in there," Kal says, changing from silent to fierce.

" Uh, I don't see how..."

"I don't care if we have to sneak in, I'm not going to be ten feet away from this game and not go!"

"Okay, okay, let me think before you do anything crazy."

The sidewalk in front is mostly empty since the game has long started. There are a few guys hanging around, and I catch the eye of one and hold up two fingers. I'd seen deals go down with scalpers on this same sidewalk when it was jam-packed before a game.

The guy says, "Fifty each, good seats."

I hold up the back of my wrist indicating I know the time, then turn over my hand to show him two twenties. We exchange tickets for cash.

His smile says, *Good for you*, but it's not friendly. My body tingles with delayed fear. I just scalped two hockey tickets. What would I do next? Oh my God, my mom would have a fit. The only thing I've ever seen her give scalpers is dirty looks.

Kal smiles wide and he really and truly looks just like Mike Kovac.

THEY'RE THE WORST TWO SEATS in the arena. I don't care. It's a relief to be in a bright, cheering crowd, watching Avilov rocket off the bench, over the boards, and onto the ice, Walt Whitman, serene in his frame, just across the street.

"Hey, where's McGill?" Kal says. "I don't see him. He's not on the ice. How come he's not skating?" He turns to the man next to him. "How come McGill's not in the game?"

"They say he's having more concussion symptoms. He's not allowed to play," the guy says. "They don't let these guys skate with the slightest sign the old coconut's not a hundred percent—long-term damage to the brain." He taps his head to show us what he means by the old coconut. "Back when I played, you took a shot to the head, they told you to shake it off, get back on the ice."

"Are you sure? I thought he was all through with that," Kal says.

The guy shrugs. "All this time after, they're still watching him like a hawk. Like I said, they treat a shot to the head real careful these days, not like it used to be."

I don't know if Kal is more upset that McGill is still hurt or that he isn't going to get to watch him play.

Truth is Avilov isn't himself either, like he was stood up for a date or something. He isn't on fire the way he would have been if his best archenemy were there.

Toward the end of the third period, Kal says, "We have to find Mother."

"He was probably the head of their group—you know, took care of things, looked out for them," I say.

"Or one crazy badass."

I don't think he was one crazy badass. I think he looks like someone's boyfriend, someone's best friend.

The Pens win even without McGill. And though I would never in a million years root for the Pittsburgh Penguins, I don't mind. It's not because the other day I had momentarily fallen in love with Nick McGill, imagining him flying his fighting kite on a windy Nova Scotia beach. It's because I watched the game through Kal's eyes.

Out in the cold spring night, Kal says, "You know, it's funny, we've spent all these years fearing Russia or the Soviet Union or whatever it was, and we were in Vietnam fighting communists—"

"And in Laos."

"And in Laos. And here's the whole city of Washington, D.C., cheering Ilya Avilov, straight out of Russia…and here's my grandfather missing, and my grandmother half-crazed, and my mother *fully* crazed *and* missing, and me wandering around not knowing where to go."

"Where *do* you go?"

"Well, I meant in the bigger sense." Kal stops. "I do have someplace to go, you know. I haven't spent any more nights sleeping at the Vietnam Wall." He says it like I would accuse him of freeloading off the federal government.

"And where is that?" I say, biting back.

"I haven't… I didn't, I didn't want you to feel bad."

"How could I feel bad about where you sleep at night?"

"Well…"

"What?"

"I'm at the STEM conference."

"*My* conference?"

"I'm pretty sure, yeah. Look, I'm sorry I didn't tell you. I'm a finalist too, which is how my grandmother let me come to D.C. by myself. The funny thing is, I was going to blow it off, same as you. I couldn't stand not seeing my grandfather's name on that wall. I just, I just wanted to go home, but there were all those kites, and then I went back to get my letter from you and you weren't there and then I missed my train and—"

"So how's it going?"

"Pretty good."

"Fine."

"What are you mad about?"

"Nothing."

"Why did you lie to me?"

"How did I lie to you?"

"By not saying."

"I didn't lie about it on purpose, it was—is something separate. I separated that from this, and it is just a highly weird coincidence that this and that have something to do with each other."

"I'm confused. Am I this or that?"

"Both?"

Kal hugs me. I'm mad but I don't know at what, so I let myself hug him back and we stand on the street between the arena and the Portrait Gallery, hanging on for dear life.

"So, you know what?" he says. "Our room is across the street from the Watergate Apartments. And guess what else, it's the room where the Watergate bad guys were, the burglars or whatever."

"Is the ghost of Richard Nixon floating around?" I think of Tomoko whispering, *Yurei.*

"I'm not afraid of Richard Nixon."

"I guess your place has a ghost just like mine."

"Any Clover sightings?"

"No, but I would like to hear from her, find out what really happened."

We agree to go home to our separate ghosts, try to find something about Mother, and meet up in Lafayette Square tomorrow.

I crashed. I was coming in same as ever and the right side of my ship started shimmying; next thing I woke up on a cot. Skip and some guy I didn't recognize were there. They were sitting around drinking and talking. Nothing broken, they said: Kovac you have an angel on your shoulder, when you see that plane, you'll know why. Said I'd been knocked out since nearly that time day before.

I started yelling for them to turn off the light, asking why it was so bright.

"Same light as ever," Skip said.

His voice was loud. It was all too loud and there were halos of light around everything. I closed my eyes and tried to go back to sleep, but there was no sleep, not then or for a long time after.

I asked how Zaj was. The three of them passed a look so when Mother started to tell me, I told him no, I understood. Zaj was dead.

CHAPTER SEVENTEEN

Mother, Poet, Poppy Fields

We do find Mother. We had both found the same thing on a memorial page dedicated to Richard "Skip" Travers. There was a note that said, *Skip Travers, you are not forgotten. Friend until the end, Fearless flyer, fearless heart. Captain Pete Motherwell, USAF.*

And I had found something Kal had not: Mother's address, or what I think is his address. If I'm right, it's two blocks from my house.

We don't call. We walk to the Metro, take it to Cleveland Park, and walk from there to his house. We're dangerously close to where I live, but I don't see anyone I know.

I've been by Mother's house a million times, seen an older couple raking leaves or planting flowers or sitting on the porch.

Kal rings the bell. The man who opens the door is the man I know. He's tall and straight as a tree with a head of messy white hair. He's old, but not an old man. Handsome.

It's him. It's Mother.

He says hello and looks at Kal, then me. He knows me, I think.

We don't, can't, speak—Kal because he's not sure and me because I am.

Finally, Kal says in a clear and grown-up voice, "I'm Kalman Kovac. My grandfather is Michael Kovac."

Mother steps back. He says, "Yes. Yes, I see."

His wife comes up behind him and peeks around. Her hair is white too, pulled back and smooth. She holds his arm and smiles in a question.

"The grandson of an old friend," says Mother. "This is Kalman Kovac and…"

I put out my hand, "Julia Bissette."

She shakes my hand and squints, like she maybe knows me. Is she gonna ask me why I'm not at camp like I'm supposed to be?

"Are you Mother?" Kal says. For all the time it took to be standing here, there is now no more time.

The woman puts the hand that's not gripping Mother's arm around the opposite shoulder.

"Captain Pete Motherwell," he says. "And yes, they called me that. Would you like to come in?"

We sit on a bright orange and green sofa in the living room. There's a baby grand piano and ceramic Chinese lamps in other bold colors. Mrs. Motherwell brings us tall glasses of ginger ale and Mother some kind of whiskey in a short glass with ice. He takes a small sip and puts it down.

Next to me is a table covered with a stiff silk cloth, the same bright green as in the sofa, with a bunch of pictures in silver frames on it. The one nearest to me is a black and white wedding photograph. The bride is wearing a simple white eyelet dress, like a slip almost. She's holding a loose bouquet of daisies down at her side, and she's barefoot. The groom is wearing a white Air Force uniform; he's wearing shoes. They're on a beach with a tall cliff behind them, and her long hair and dress are blowing in the wind. Mother's holding his hat tight to his side with one hand; the other one is holding hers.

"We met when I was back here in Washington," Mother says when he sees me looking at the picture. He turns to his wife who'd been standing there, but she's slipped out of the room.

"He's not on the Wall and he's not home," Kal says. He leans forward in his chair, his voice an accusation.

Mother doesn't flinch. "I knew Mike Kovac," he says. He was a fine pilot and a fine man, and…a great friend. I don't forget him."

Kal waits for him to elaborate. Wide bands of sunlight cross over the room in lines and angles. I'm not here to speak. And yet, after a long silence, I do. "Can you tell us anything else?"

Mother takes a deep breath in through his nose and gently lets it go.

"Poet," that's what we called him. "He was a great pilot, son, I'm telling you a great pilot and decent and—this word gets tossed around a lot, but—he was a brave man, and a good friend. He was all that."

"Was he a Raven?" says Kal.

"No, though they had him up with us for a while, he was practically one of us, but he was different."

"How different?"

"He was in uniform. We Ravens left our gear at Udorn. Any-thing to call us military—ID, tags, flight suit—all that was left behind. We aren't Air Force for a while, we have Embassy IDs, Lao drivers' licenses. We're there for the Ambassador, helping out. Do you see? There's no war, but we're fighting a war. We go around in unmarked planes and vehicles. There's no Americans fighting in Laos, but we're there.

"We weren't involved in the bigger picture, but Poet was. He stayed with us for a while, and we got to know him. Anybody else, we might think he was sent over to keep track of us—but, Poet, he wasn't that.

"He flew back and forth to Vientiane a lot. I think he used to swap out books with some folks at the Embassy. He did a lot of reading and a lot of writing, but we called him Poet more to the way he saw things.

"We understood ourselves fine, but if you took a step back or if you were looking in from the outside, you might not understand. We were fighting a war where there could be no war. Laos was a neutral country. The NVA and the Pathet Lao were trying to take things over, and we were trying to prevent that. You had the Ho Chi Minh Trail, a supply route that connected North and South Vietnam but it ran through Laos, that was part of the reason."

He stopped and then said, "CIA, U.S. Embassy, the Palace, the Hmong and their general—Vang Pao. There were a lot of moving pieces in that puzzle. Your grandfather fit together with all those things, but he wasn't any one of those things. If it was hard for him, he didn't show it. He worked long hours. We all did. We flew out of a secret airport, Lima 20 Alternate, until an attack closed that down and then we flew out of Vientiane. He was with us there too. It was the dry season and we were commuting up to the PDJ.

"The PDJ," says Kal. "The Plain of Jars."

"Yes."

"He talked about that."

Mother looks at him.

"In his log, his journal," says Kal. "I was, uh, given it recently."

Mother absorbs this without expression. "It was a sacred place, lost, won, and lost—the PDJ," he says.

How does dropping bombs on a place keep it sacred? I think, but have the sense to keep quiet. Mother knows things I don't.

"Poet, his backseat man was Zaj," says Mother. "I remember those two patching up their 01 after a day of flying. That's how it was, we'd get shot up and we'd patch up our plane until it wouldn't patch anymore.

"The terrain is unforgiving. A downed man, uncaptured, couldn't last more than three days in that jungle. A captured man is a missing man.

"How can there be prisoners of war where there is no war? Not one American prisoner was ever released or negotiated for. The end of the war was a complicated bundle of bargains. The missing men in Laos were not part of that bargain. None came home. We're not letting that go, though, we're still trying. Men alive in Laos? It's possible. I've heard the Lao say, 'tens of tens.'"

"Who's we?"

"Some of us."

Again, I resist the urge to speak. I want to stand up and yell, *Tell us what happened, I can see that you know, why won't you tell?* Gravity keeps me in my seat—the gravity of his words as much as the gravity of the earth.

Mother looks at me and says, "You are his friend?" Meaning Kal.

"Yes."

"And my neighbor, I take it?"

"Yes."

He picks up his glass and takes a small sip. He's fit and composed, not that kind of shaky old man you see sometimes.

"Poet and Zaj crashed," he says. That plane was patched so many times… We brought Zaj's body to the village.

"There are things we now know that we didn't know back then. We know that a man can suffer an injury that's not a broken

139

bone. A man's spirit can be broken—or, as the Hmong say, his soul can be stolen. Your grandfather saw poetry in the world, and you might say that made him vulnerable, but son, that is not the case. It was the opposite. It made him strong. I am living witness to that. He was an uncommon man.

"We thought the reason he was so changed is that he lost his backseater. They were close. But Poet had an injury you couldn't see to fix or amputate. He was nervous about his vision—I remember that. He kept asking to get it checked. He was a pilot. But the tests came out fine. Whatever was bothering him about his sight, they couldn't find it."

He pauses.

"Kalman, your grandfather, Mike Kovac—Poet—carried on. He was injured in a way no one knew but he kept on."

"What happened to him? Did he die?"

"There was heroin everywhere. You could say the CIA and Vang Pao were part of it, or they turned a blind eye to it—a lot of people have a lot to say about it—but one thing's for sure, when they started sending Number 4 heroin to the streets of Saigon, they had a captive audience of young men far from home."

"What happened? What does that have to do with it?" Kal says. "Is that how he died?"

"No, son. He didn't die. He came home."

Kal, defying grief and gravity, stands up. "HOW DO YOU KNOW?"

"I know he came home because I was with him. We flew from Udorn, Thailand, to Andrews Air Force Base. Together."

"Why won't you tell me what happened?" says Kal, sitting down again, his voice fragile and pleading. "Why won't you tell me the truth?"

"That is what happened. That is the truth."

"Did you talk to him? Did he say anything to you on the plane?"

"There was talk about Alaska. They were building the pipeline, for oil, and there was pilot work. I know some men went there to disappear. Not everyone that made it back made it home. It was a different time. It's hard to imagine for you but it was a different time."

"Did he say he was going to Alaska?" Kal asks, his voice, finally, broken.

"No, he didn't. He said he was going home."

Kal puts his elbows on his knees, his face in his hands, and cries.

Mother and I sit in that bright and beautiful room and wait.

He cries a long time. When it seems like he might stop crying, I move over on the sofa and put my arm around him. He doesn't shake me off.

"There's something else," says Mother.

He waits, and finally Kal says, "What else?"

"After spending so much time in and around Long Tieng, he got to know the locals well. We all did; we worked side by side with them. There were a lot of friendships."

He looks at us like he might just leave it at that. Mrs. Motherwell comes in from somewhere and stands with her hands clasped.

"It's all right, Penny," he says. "We're fine," and she leaves.

"There were poppy fields, in the hills—opium. Policy came down to clear them out. That was his last flying, spraying those fields. The herbicide they used, Agent Orange, destroyed them."

"Destroyed the people?" I ask.

"The poppies, but it made them sick, the locals. We'd seen it before when they were using it on the rice. Now we know even more, what that chemical has done to so many of our vets, but we knew something then. Mike knew."

Kal makes a noise, a gasp, the sound you make when gravity is pulling you into the earth.

"I'm sorry," says Mother. "It was very, very difficult. A man falls down a well, he can hear his friends calling, but he can't make it back out of that well. I could guess the reasons he couldn't get back home, but I don't know, really."

"What about Skip Travers? What about him?" I say, though the gravity is making it hard.

"Tens of tens," says Mother.

Two long weeks with this deep, sharp pain in my head—I can't shake it. It starts in my right eye and stabs inward to the center of my brain and there's no letting up.

Sleep and awake are a tangle and everything's still glowing halos: trees, mountains, piles of garbage, everything. Even Mother had a halo of light around his dirty, unshaven face. He sat down, put his arm around me, and said something about me having passed the physical and that I was good to fly.

I'm so relieved. I flew myself into this place and I sure as hell am going to fly myself out.

CHAPTER EIGHTEEN

Memorial Bridge, Late at Night

Back at the hotel, everything is awful. I can't shake our time with Mother. I feel weird in my swanky hotel, across the street from the president of the United States. I think about Kal in his dorm at GW, across the street from the Watergate, the unintentional monument to a ripped-off nation. I'm glad I'm not contracting a foot fungus, but I'm envious. I know I'm missing out on something.

I lie in bed and stare at the ceiling; it really is quite a ceiling. I fall asleep and dream about Clover.

We're sitting at the dining table in my suite, the one Kal had laid the blood chit on. There's a fire in the fireplace and we're drinking from translucent china teacups with blue flowers.

"Just tea," she says with a laugh, and I know she means not poison. We're close friends and talk all the time about how and where you would do it.

"It's your own life," I say, "to do with what you want." It's funny I say this to her, because my mom says it to me all the time but now it means something different. It means I don't hold it against her for drinking photography chemicals and dying. But the way she looks at me, I can tell she knows I wish she hadn't done it.

"It's the same with my aunt," she says. "Now my husband's cup, I can't vouch for," she says with a giggle.

And then it's Clover and me sitting on a bench at her gravesite, but it's Mike Kovac's grave. I say, "This statue is for Mike Kovac."

"Who is Mike Kovac?" she says.

I tell her he's a friend of mine—a soldier and a poet. "When the time comes, he'll take your statue, and you can have the hillside looking out over his valley in Ohio."

She asks where he is now, and I say I don't know.

"My old friends, John and Clara Hay, are at the Lakeview Cemetery in Cleveland, Ohio. Now that is a beautiful place."

"Okay, Cleveland, I'll make sure you get to Cleveland."

In my dream I'm happy because I'm setting things right. Clover is smiling because she'll be near John and Clara. I'm trying to say something still isn't right with Mike Kovac, but there's buzzing.

"Hold on, it's my phone," I say.

She says she understands.

I wake up. It's late and dark, past midnight. My phone is buzzing and vibrating. It's a bunch of one-word texts from Kal.

Out

Here

On

The

ON THE WHAT? I text back.

Bridge

Where? I quit with the capital letters. I don't want to shout-text him off any bridge.

Between Lincoln and the graves

What, what, what is he doing on the bridge? I think I know, but I don't want to know. I lie there for a minute. Then I move fast. I slip out of the hotel and take a cab to Ohio Drive. The driver shakes his head at the late hour and deserted spot by the Potomac where he lets me out. I run up the huge set of stairs that go to the back of the Lincoln Memorial and then over and onto the bridge. I don't want to think anything, but I'm thinking everything. My lungs are burning fire by the time I reach Kal—he's halfway to Arlington, sitting on the stone railing, holding his hands out wide. He waves easily, as if he isn't ten stories up. The Potomac is a black shiny reflection of the cold night sky.

"Air Force Memorial," says Kal, pointing to the silver arcs all lit up. It's still far away, but it's a good view from here. My mouth is so dry I can't swallow and my hands are shaking. *I spy something silver*, I say to myself to try and calm down. I miss my dad. I could use his help right now.

"Moment of inertia," says Kal. Arlington Cemetery glows at one end of the bridge; the giant stone box holding Lincoln at the other.

"Yes. Please don't move, Kal." When I say it, I pretend I'm Suzy. I pretend my husband is lost and my daughter is gone and my grandson—my sweet, funny, beautiful grandson—is balancing on a tightrope. I pretend that I love him so much that all the thoughts in my brain will keep him from falling.

"It doesn't mean that," Kal says, annoyed. "Moment of inertia is about rotational motion—a rotating rigid body maintains its state of uniform motion." He moves his hand in a circle to show me a rotating rigid body in uniform motion.

"STEM camp?"

"Suzy has a spinning wheel, an old-fashioned one, like in a fairy tale. When I was little, I worried she would prick her finger on the spindle and sleep for a thousand years, but it wasn't the story of Sleeping Beauty, it was Rumpelstiltskin. He came and took her firstborn.

"It works by a treadle you pump with your foot. She uses the wool from our sheep to make yarn. I used to sit with a giant pile of carded wool on my lap and hand it up to her... so you see..." he says, with an embarrassed laugh, "I'm a long way from home."

"Would you please come down from there?" I hold out my hand. *I'm Suzy*, I think. *I love you, Kalman Kovac. I love you. You have brought me years and years of joy and relief from my suffering. I am your grandmother and I love you and I won't let you go.*

"I made a flywheel," he says. "It keeps a light powered even after you finish working the crank. That's my entry. A thousand hours, I watched that spinning wheel spin. I saw how the flywheel stored energy from the treadle."

"A flywheel, I like it."

"It doesn't matter anymore."

"Why not?"

"I'm done."

I don't want to know what that means. I do know that if I grab his arm and pull, he'll pull me back and go over, taking me with him. I do know grief and gravity win a lot of the time.

"Hey, I say. I'm not Suzy anymore; I'm me again, a kid who can't fix anything. "Lincoln's right there." It comes out like, *You can't kill yourself in front of Lincoln*—which sounds ridiculous, but honestly, that's what I mean.

"Are you a freak? It's a statue in a box."

"Come down, okay?"

"I came here to find my grandfather but the more I find, the less I understand."

"I made a fractal," I say, because I want him to know how much I need him to be okay and that I trust him. "That I was too cool or scared or angry to give my presentation makes me wonder what in the world will become of me." I don't know if he wants to hear about my fractal, but it's the most honest thing I can think of. "I wish I'd given my speech is all."

Kal doesn't answer, but for the first time since I arrived on the bridge, his eyes acknowledge me.

"Your flywheel. That sounds good," I say.

"My presentation is tomorrow."

"Can I come?"

"Yes. Please. I want you to. Promise me you'll be there."

"Promise me *you'll* be there."

"Of course I'll be there. I'm showing my flywheel, for the prize." He hops off the stone railing like he's not on a bridge at all. He's pretending it's not cold and late and I haven't lost my mind making sure he's okay.

We walk back over the bridge, but I keep away from him. My head is buzzing. I'm shaking. If he notices, he doesn't say anything.

We climb up onto the back porch of the Lincoln Memorial. I sit on the edge, dangling my feet, but I'm too jittery to keep them still. I smack my heels into the marble hard, first one, then the other. Smack. Smack. Smack.

Kal sits down right up next to me. He smacks his heels against the marble too, in rhythm with mine. Smack, smack, smack.

We look out at the river, the bridge, Arlington Cemetery.

"Why would they face him that way?" Kal says.

"Who?"

"Lincoln, with his back to the soldiers."

"A mistake, I guess."

They sent me back down to Udorn to wait for my orders.

My head is a constellation of pain. The pills they gave me don't help. If Zaj were alive, he'd bring me a pinch from his opium ball.

I wear my Ray-Bans day and night now, outdoors and indoors. I don't even take them off when I lie down to try and sleep.

I keep asking to be checked and keep passing the vision test so I remain clear to fly.

CHAPTER NINETEEN

Flywheel

Tomoko isn't sitting on George Washington's hat, but she practically is. She's got her arm around the big man himself. "Don't even think about kissing him," I shout. "I mean it." Her face is right up next to his and she's clicking off a stream of selfies. We're behind the Lisner Auditorium waiting to see Kal's presentation.

There are a lot of statues of George Washington around town, but this one is the best. He's a soldier. He's sitting on a bench with his Revolutionary War hat—the one Tomoko is on—to his side. One hand is on his knee and the other is holding his sword, its point resting on the pavement. He doesn't have that weird haircut and sour look you see on the dollar. His expression says he's going to try his best to do a good job.

Like falling in love with Nick McGill, falling in love with a statue of George Washington is crazy. But this time feeling crazy makes me mad. Maybe it's the way Tomoko is mauling him, taking shot after shot, each one with a different expression. Thank God, George is keeping it real with his steady gaze.

"Come on," I say, "we're gonna be late."

We sit in the back row of the auditorium. No one knows me, but I still want to be invisible. Kal comes on the stage and talks about his flywheel. It's impressive. There's a lot of applause when he finishes. Then something terrible happens.

My name is called.

"We have one more presenter," the man at the podium says. Kal, who's next to him, shades his eyes and looks out. He sees me and waves me forward.

He whispers something to the moderator, then comes down off the stage and walks to the back of the room, stands at the end of my aisle, and again waves me forward. The kids in the audience crane their necks to see what's going on.

I look at Tomoko. She doesn't know I'm supposed to be here in the first place. I never told her that little detail, but she's encouraging me to go on, stand up. Defy gravity. I stand up. When I get to Kal, I whisper, "Are you kidding me? I don't have my stuff. I'm going to kill you." I consider bolting for the door.

"They have your submission, you know what you did. Now come on."

He takes my hand and walks me to the stage. I'm thinking how to travel back in time ten minutes and not be here at all. Then I see it, a guy working a video setup. I'm not prepared, it's gonna be terrible, but I will have videographic proof of my presence at this year's Elite STEM Conference. I need this. I'm still mad at Kal—even though this is saving my butt, I'm still mad. Extremely.

My presentation (from the video):

*Umm, so, yeah, my name is Julia—umm, Bissette. I'm from...
here, (laughter) Washington, D.C. My um, presentation is on,
uh, fractals. Fractal geometry.*

I look out at the audience. There are maybe four hundred
kids, some adults too. I'm thinking how crazy irked I am at Kal for
blindsiding me. He wants to beat me at STEM, so he can pretend
I didn't talk him off the bridge last night. I know that's insane, but
I also know how it is with people. So much has happened between
us. I thought he was different, but standing here, I'm sure he is not.

I wonder what feats of STEM the kids in the audience had
conjured to be here, and then I remember that I'm only one of
five. I'm a finalist. They're here to see me—or maybe their parents
think Science, Technology, Engineering, and Math is résumé
froth the way my mom does. Maybe they don't want to be here
at all. This makes me madder. I *do* want to be here. I worked
hours and hours on this project and it wasn't to make my mom
or anybody happy.

On the video, you see me staring out for an awkward amount
of time, and you hear people starting to fidget in their seats.
Someone giggles. I'm thinking, *You wished for this last night
and you got your wish.* I'm also thinking about the guy taking
professional video and how I could send it to my mom and dad.

I continue.

*Geometry helps us measure the physical world. Measuring a
thing is a way of understanding it. Fractal geometry is a way
to measure things we didn't think we could, things with rough
edges like the coast of England, a cloud, a Yoshino cherry tree
in full bloom. You can make fractals on a computer and you
can find them in nature.*

*I got the idea of combining the two from staring at the bare tree
outside my bedroom and thinking about how when it blooms*

it's the best and most beautiful time in Washington, D.C. I'm sorry it's so cold. Usually the cherry blossoms are here by now.

I like the planes and shapes and proofs of formal geometry but I love fractal geometry, which makes possible what we thought was impossible.

A fractal is a thing that is itself over and over again, infinitely. Like looking at yourself in a three-way mirror. No matter how small the piece, it still contains a complete representation of the whole.

My fractal is a computer graphic I made using an L-system. An L-system is like a set of rules in a string; it has a recursive function—it repeats itself—which is perfect for creating fractals.

L-systems were developed in the late 1960s by a botanist from Hungary named Aristid Lindenmayer. He wanted to model the growth of plants.

I started with several turtles because I wanted to make lots of trees blooming at once. A turtle is how you translate computer language into a picture. It's not a real turtle, but imagine a real turtle holding a pen—the program tells him where to draw next.

I glance back and see my program on the screen behind me, the trunks of the trees, iterating and blooming. I look out at the auditorium. I'm wondering if there really are this many people in the world interested in the things I'm interested in.

Fractals interest me for their beauty, surprise, and infinite nature. Unlike a star or a plant or a person, they don't have a birth, a life, or a death; they never end.

Thank you.

There's a lot of clapping, not flimsy clapping, but good loud clapping. They're clapping for me and for my fully bloomed cherry trees.

I bow politely and step down from the podium, walk off the stage and out the first door I find. I follow Exit signs through a hallway where I find the actual Exit and open the door into bright sunlight. My phone buzzes. I turn it off.

Long light waves hit the molecules and particles in the air. The sky is bluer than a Tiffany box, bluer than all the skies in the paintings at the National Gallery, bluer than the view from a plane over Lima 20 Alternate. It's the most real and perfect blue I've ever seen in my life.

I walk over to the big Albert Einstein statue to look at his kind face. I think about how the c in $E = mc^2$ refers to light in a vacuum, which is a theoretical kind of light, and how the speed of light in air, water, and glass is a real kind of light.

I stand on the same spot where Kal had shouted his name when I told him there'd be an echo.

"Why am I here?" I call out to Einstein.

"Am I here?" he answers.

I have sworn so many oaths and still I swear one more. I will find my way back to you.

You are standing barefoot on the porch, Suzanne, when a soldier drives up to the house. You are standing on the porch, shading your eyes from the afternoon sun. I'm keeping myself alive so no soldier except me will come to our house.

We'll sit on the hill and listen to the evening. The sun leans toward the horizon, showing me the colors in your eyes, the shades and patterns that are for me alone.

We fought, you and I, I didn't forget. There was a day we fought and didn't speak for the rest of that day and night, and I would give anything for that day and night back.

If there was a moment you thought I was not a man in this world who would do anything for the woman in this world who made that man, I couldn't, I wouldn't...I could not bear it.

CHAPTER TWENTY

A Gift from the People of Japan

At the Hay-Adams, I walk through the lobby in my usual way, confident, no slinking around. I'm nearly through when I hear my name. It's the woman at the front desk. She waves me over, holding her arm high like a teacher who wants to speak to you privately.

"There's something here for you."

I wait.

She waits.

Like I say, I have skills—I'd wait all day, but my first order of business is not attracting attention to myself, so I let her win our second little face-off and say, "May I have it?"

She hands me the letter. It's so beautiful, I resent her hands even touching it. The paper is more translucent than the china teacups in my dream of Clover, but for its translucence it's surprisingly heavy. It's addressed to me, *Julia Bissette, The Hay-Adams Hotel*, in calligraphy equal to the paper it's written on.

In the suite, I lay it carefully on the table, where Mike Kovac's blood chit had been, where I had sat and read his journal, where I had sipped tea with Clover.

The fireplace has three birch logs in it, but doesn't work. Even so, I sit down next to it as I imagine Clover had when she drank photography chemicals, and think about Mike Kovac.

"Mike," I say, "it's about Kal, your grandson. We're competing for the same prize and he forced me to give my presentation when I wasn't prepared. That was after waking me up in the middle of the night for a get-together on the Memorial Bridge. I feel tricked. I don't know if we found you or not. I wonder what's in the letter.

"Mike, do you know Clover? She killed herself by drinking chemicals. What happened to you?"

I consider ordering afternoon tea to have with Clover, but that's the sort of thing a crazy person or a child would do. I am neither.

I open my letter. It's an invitation—to tea. Not just to tea, but to a tea ceremony at the Japanese Embassy. Clover had a hand in this. It's a thought even too abstract for fractal geometry.

I write a note back on the hotel stationary. It's thick, heavy, creamy paper with the Hay-Adams crest on the top. It might be the nicest stationary, I've ever seen if I hadn't just opened my invitation from the Embassy of Japan. I use the pen in the holder on the desk. I say, *I'd be delighted to attend*, in my best handwriting, address it to the Embassy, and call for someone to come and mail it for me.

I haven't called anyone for anything before this. But I have gone past the world of flywheels and fractals to living in a painting—not ballet dancers on a stage, but an *onna bugeisha* in battle. I have drunk tea with Clover. I have delivered a baby with

Mike Kovac. I have accepted an invitation from the Embassy of Japan just as William Sturgis Bigelow surely had. And since I have done all these things, I most certainly can call the concierge to come up and mail my letter.

I get a text from Tomoko asking if she can stop by.

Please come. I write back.

A few minutes later, I open the door to an enormous box with a pair of legs and feet in delicate pink sandals.

"This is for you," the box says and hands itself to me. Tomoko emerges from behind it.

I put it down and turn to her. We bow to each other. The box is as pretty and white as a wedding cake.

"I—I can't," I say.

Tomoko gestures with her small hand. "It would be my pleasure." Pleasure came out with the smallest lilt of an *r*, *preasure*. Not a cartoon of a Japanese person talking, but delicate and fine.

In the box is a kimono. It's pale orange and cream silk, with a geometric star pattern. Underneath it is an obi, the sash. It's green with a leaf design. Beneath the kimono and the obi, wrapped separately, are Japanese sandals and socks.

"From the People of Japan," says Tomoko.

It's a gift for me, from a whole country, and a girl, and her father—the man who had followed the trail of William Sturgis Bigelow to Amayashi and brought her to the National Gallery of Art. I fall under its spell.

I think of Kal and feel the fairy-tale spindle prick of a story coming undone, because I only want to wear that kimono and go to a tea ceremony at the Embassy of Japan.

I don't want to worry about Mike Kovac anymore. I had pictured him, old and sick in Alaska, or somewhere in the Lower 48, like one of those guys up on Rockville Pike, with a cardboard sign, *Vietnam Vet, Please Help*. I had pictured his injured brain, reinjured to where he can't remember that anyone still cares about him or how to get home. I had pictured him dead, not buried in Arlington Cemetery, but dead with no grave, no anything.

I put all these pictures out of my head. I can't change possible outcomes, so better to see him leaning on his weapon in Ray-Bans in the pulsing light of a hot afternoon in Southeast Asia.

I want my old hair back. I want long hair to my feet and to wear layers of silk robes and play Go with Tomoko in Kyoto a thousand years ago, even before the Heike and the Genji went to war and Amayashi died by her own sword and cousin's hand.

"I need to make an appointment," I say to Tomoko. She knows I mean my hair and pulls off the delicate trick of agreeing with me without insulting me.

⌁

THE CUT AND COLOR IS four hundred and fifty dollars, which I put on my dad's card. Neither I, nor the woman swiping the card, flutter a pulse. Not being where you're supposed to be, backing out on things you said you'd follow through on, credit card theft—these kinds of things get easier as you go along.

The color is exactly right. The foot of hair that had gone out with the hotel trash can't be immediately replaced, but I like the cut. Tomoko gets a manicure and pedicure while I sit with my head covered in tinfoil. The Speaker of the House is here; also a TV reporter I recognize; there are some garden-variety society skeletons, and whoever else gets their hair colored at the top salon in Washington. I'm getting my blowout when Tomoko asks about Kal. I can't hear, but her mouth says, "Where is Kal?"

I shrug. I want back the person I was before I met Kal, a person who could represent their country to a visitor from Japan, a lover of Abraham Lincoln and Walt Whitman, a person of science.

There's a poem I know that I can't remember.

On the far-stretching beauteous landscape, the roads and lanes...

CHAPTER TWENTY-ONE

A Kite Is a Victim

'm named after a fractal," I say through the bathroom door. Kal is in there, in the tub. He had asked if he could take a bath, and I had said yes, if he promised to lock the door. It didn't make any sense, asking him to lock me out, but I had wanted a condition, just because. The other day I had given the housekeeper twenty dollars to get rid of the decomposing clothes, so I didn't have a reason to say no.

He had been calling since this morning. There were texts and messages on my phone; even the hotel room phone was blinking. I hadn't left the room or answered the phone. I couldn't bring myself to do it. He seemed so regular all of a sudden, and I was afraid I might be rude.

Most recently he had texted DOWNSTAIRS, which I ignored, then he texted Talking to Ashley, which I did not ignore.

I picked up the hotel phone, called the front desk, and, in as brisk a voice as I could muster, asked to please send up our guest.

Ashley—she had said "This is Ashley," upon answering—said, "*Our?*"

I hung up. Again, her job was to do what I said, no further instructions necessary.

"My old friend," Kal said when I answered the door. He meant my hair; it was back to the color it was the day we met.

"Bought and paid for." I too meant my hair. But I also meant all of me. My whole self was bought and paid for. My dad, my mom, Cabbage, the shrink, Ashley—there was money between all of us. Even my friends at school had been purchased, in a way, selected for me to associate with by the mere fact that our parents could afford the tuition.

Except my cousin Chloe, she and I were free to each other. Though… maybe that's why my aunt moved away, maybe she didn't want to be on the family payroll anymore. And who knows, maybe that was my mom's beef way back when. To me, my grandmother is perfect, but she runs the show. I honestly hadn't ever thought there was a good reason for my mom splitting up with my dad. Now as I look at it, it occurs to me that she might have had one. It could have been anything. What if, for instance, my dad didn't want her to be a lawyer, like Henry Adams didn't want Clover to publish her photographs? I'm not saying that was the case, but considering the possibility was new.

"I know, you said," Kal says in response to me telling him I'm a fractal.

"I didn't think you'd remember."

"I remember."

"A Julia Set—get it? Julia Bissette."

"Yeah, I get it. Why'd he do that? I mean it's extremely cool, but how'd he know to name you after a fractal?"

"He wanted to have something over on my mom, I guess, a secret, you know. Plus he was supposed to be some kind of genius math guy but ended up just making a lot of cash on Wall Street…yeah, epic fail."

"Epic's too strong." Kal is sticking up for my dad. I appreciate it.

"He still does some cool stuff—chaos theory, that kind of thing."

"What's that?"

"It's like, can the flap of a butterfly's wings in Brazil set off a tornado in Texas. Small disturbances can have monumental outcomes. Same with a Julia Set, it's a fractal that's made a small change of plans. Instead of repeating itself over and over, it becomes something else entirely. It's a wild and beautiful fractal."

"Like you."

I don't answer. After a while I say, "You never told me the poem."

"What poem?"

"The one that was instead of a lullaby."

"I know that's what you meant."

I wait.

"I saw the paintings," Kal says after a while. "The ones Tomoko's father found. Hey, I've been sleeping under Kintaro and a carp my whole life. I'm interested."

"What do you think?"

"I like the one where she's riding into battle. I like them all."

"Same." I want to hear the poem, but I'm not asking twice. I lay my head down on the floor and wait. There are small splashing sounds, like he's smacking the top of the water with the palm of his hand.

"A kite is a victim you are sure of," he says.

You love it because it pulls
gentle enough to call you master,
strong enough to call you fool;
because it lives
like a desperate trained falcon
in the high sweet air,
and you can always haul it down
to tame it in your drawer.

"Okay?" he says.
"Okay. Is that all of it?"
"No."
"Can I hear the rest?"

A kite is a fish you have already caught
in a pool where no fish come,
so you play him carefully and long,
and hope he won't give up,
or the wind die down.

A kite is the last poem you've written,
so you give it to the wind,
but you don't let it go
until someone finds you
something else to do.

He stops. I don't say anything and he continues.

A kite is a contract of glory
that must be made with the sun,
so make friends with the field
the river and the wind,
then you pray the whole cold night before,
under the travelling cordless moon,
to make you worthy and lyric and pure.

I lay on the floor, seeing not the elaborate ceiling of the Hay-Adams but the kite painting of Kintaro, brave and strong, and the carp, pushing against the current to lay her eggs.

Kal says, "That's the end."

I stay silent.

"The ending part is the part she said every night. It was only one night, the last night, that she said anything about a kite being a victim."

"What happened that night?"

"I grew up."

"Brave and strong?"

"Well...I was prepared the next day when she was gone."

I admit to myself that I'd been lying when I said Kal suddenly seemed regular.

We stay like that a long time, Kal floating in the still water, me suspended in the kite-flying air.

"Kal," I say, "I'm tired." And I am, more tired than I can ever remember being.

"I don't know any lullabies."

"Just the one poem?"

"Just the one poem."

"That would be good."

He tells me the kite poem.

When he gets to the end, I say, "Again."

⚶

IN THE MORNING, HE'S GONE. I had fallen asleep on the floor in the hallway outside the bathroom door.

There's a note on the table, written on a piece of Hay-Adams stationary. *Bye, Julia. Thanks for letting me take a bath.* It's signed *Kalman Kovac.* Below that, there's an arrow pointing to a tiny box kite. It's made from a Nerds Rope wrapper, cut and folded, with wooden coffee stirrers for supports.

Under the pointing arrow it says, *I fly.*

I go to the window and open it, letting in the cold April wind. I hold onto the thread and let the air catch the small kite. It's true.

And along the edge of the sky, in the horizon's far margin.

CHAPTER TWENTY-TWO

My Kimono, My Capture

Tomoko and I play Go. I told her I wanted to learn, and she arrived at my door with a small fold-up board and a bag of black and white stones. I caught on fast, but she's good. I thought her Japanese manners might let me win. I tease her about her ruthless play, and she says, "I would never insult you, Julia, with not my best game."

The more games we play, the more I see the possibilities and that the strategies really are endless. We play until it's time to get ready for the Embassy. She shows me how to put the kimono on, ties the obi for me, and leaves.

I sit in one of the dining chairs very still, not wanting to disturb a thing. I'm an iteration not of myself, but of Tomoko the first time I saw her. I hold my phone in both hands. It doesn't buzz. I have nothing for anyone and no one has anything for me.

Did Clover sit in a kimono brought back from Kyoto by her cousin William Sturgis Bigelow? Would he describe the tea ceremony to her the way Tomoko described it to me, a sacred pursuit of harmony, respect, purity, and tranquility? I want all these things—will I find them in a cup of tea? The kimono makes me think so.

John and Clara Hay would be there too. John Hay—Abraham Lincoln's personal secretary, who helped with his correspondence and made him laugh and was with him when he died—she had a friend like that and still it wasn't enough.

Suddenly, I'm not an iteration of Tomoko, but of Clover. I understand why she loved photography. It's about light—how much, how fast, how straight, how bent. It's laying things down on paper in measures of light and dark.

She punished her husband with her absence and he punished her back with a monument not to her light but to her absence of light.

I'm Clover, a kite on a string, high and beautiful and admired. Yet I only go where someone else decides. I'm Clover and I don't want to be. I don't want to be a desperate, trained falcon. I don't want to be hauled down and tamed in a drawer.

Very slowly, so I don't disrupt my kimono or my beautifully tied obi or my D.C. VIP blowout, I pack my things to go.

AT THE FRONT DESK, ASHLEY and I have one last stare-down. All week she's been watching me like a jay, yet now I'm supposed to believe that she doesn't notice that I'm wearing a kimono. "I'd like to check out, please," I say and hand her my card. Her pink polished nails tip tap on her keyboard.

She smiles, not the hotel smile she's been dishing out all week, but the smile of someone who thinks they know, when they don't know. "Would you excuse me for one minute?"

I smile a calm, kimono-wearing smile back. I'm happy to be leaving and to never feel her thinly disguised curiosity and fake hospitality again.

Serene with courtesy and that leaving feeling when you know it really is time to go, I have all the time in the world for her to finish her hotel busywork.

I don't have leather armor and a horse, a twin cousin nearby to cut off my head, or even photography chemicals. I have the dignity of the People of Japan. I am wearing my gift from them when Ashley tells me my credit card has been declined.

I'm breathing, but I'm not getting any air. It's happening faster than I can make it stop. I'm going to have to call my dad and ask him to pay the bill.

Less and less air is traveling to my brain. I have to move my body. It's the only way. I'm flooding with adrenalin. I have to exert myself to breath again. It's the fight-or-flight gift from my caveman ancestors to save me from a saber-toothed tiger, but I am wearing a kimono, and Japanese socks and clogs. I can only take very small steps, so that's what I do. I take small urgent steps all the way to the door. I can't explain that I need to move so I can breathe and that I'm not going to flee.

A thousand tiny steps later, I reach the door. The doorman blocks my way. I motion for him to let me out. He shakes his head no. I motion again. It looks like he's going to grab my arm, and I cannot let him touch my kimono. This is what I'm thinking when I pick up a beautiful and enormous vase of flowers. My intention is to hand it to him. My oxygen-deprived brain thinks, *Here, take this and I'll just sneak by while you're figuring out how not to drop it.*

I wrap my arms around the vase and tilt it toward me, but it's too heavy to lift. I know I do not want to ruin my kimono, so I push it away from me. For a long moment, it looks like it will tilt itself back upright.

Then it crashes to the ground.

I don't yell, or gesticulate, or grenade them with curse words, but I do refuse to come along.

When they cuff me, I don't go limp like a White House protester, in honor of my gift from the People of Japan. I don't give over to the cops, in honor of Tomoko, who had so recently taught me that anything less than my best effort would be an insult to my fellow man, cops or otherwise.

※

AT THE POLICE STATION, I call Cabbage.

Captain Willingham comes in.

I want his face to register bemusement or disappointment, but it shows nothing. For the second time in his presence, I force hot tears away. He unlocks the handcuffs and gives them to the officer who had put them on. He holds my wrists in his large hands and sighs, like a father looking at a daughter he does not know what to do with.

"My lawyer's on her way," I say.

"Okay."

"We found out about Kal's grandfather." I want to tell him everything I know about Mike Kovac and have him assure me everything's going to be okay, that Mike Kovac is okay, that I'm okay, but I had lawyered up. The conversation is over.

Nor do I forget you, departed.

CHAPTER TWENTY-THREE
An App for Go

S ome of it is fixed with money. My father pays my hotel
bill and clears up the problem with his credit card in one
short phone call. He compensates the hotel for their vase,
which they claim is some kind of artifact. I hope with all my hope
that it wasn't a gift to Clover from William Sturgis Bigelow.

The People of Japan had given me a kimono and invited
me to tea and I didn't go. This couldn't be fixed with money.
When I tell Tomoko I had been arrested, her eyes widen with
the adventure of it and she asks if there's a picture. I have to
smile at that.

She lies to her dad and says I wasn't feeling well. I don't want a
lie to come between the person who discovered the lost paintings
of Amayashi and me. He is the closest thing to William Sturgis

Bigelow and Clover on this earth. My heart aches to think about it. Tomoko puts her arm around me and says, "It will still be nice between you and my father, Julia, but your sorrow is correct."

The car and driver that had taken us to the 9:30 Club and the CIA takes Tomoko and me to Dulles Airport. The scrolls of Amayashi are returning to Japan in the hold of the plane that Tomoko is about to board. Her father isn't leaving for another week and is trusting Tomoko with this sacred mission. She is honored and, because he trusts me to escort her, even if it's only to the airport, I'm honored. I hadn't expected another chance so soon.

At the security gate she doesn't say goodbye or even look back. She takes off her shoes and puts them with her giant purse and her phone in a gray plastic bin. She puts the bin on the conveyor belt to be x-rayed. On the other side, she puts on her shoes, picks up her stuff, and texts me as she heads toward the gate.

There is an app for Go. Simple to learn.

A lifetime to master. I write back.

There's no telling what else those flying thumbs have in store for me, this minute, next year, in fifty years. We're different in every way, yet we have become each other's mirror image with a simple bow. *For every atom belonging to me as good belongs to you.*

Tomoko texts me all through her flight and hasn't stopped since. My mom is funny. Instead of saying, "Who are you talking to?" all exasperated like she usually does when I'm on my phone at weird hours, if she thinks it's Tomoko, she gets kind of satisfied and happy. She likes the idea of me having an international friend or something. I think she fell under the spell of the kimono hanging in my room—and who could blame her.

I hear from Kal too. After getting off the train in Cleveland, he sends me a picture of a statue. It's an angel with huge wings, a helmet and a sword, and the serpent he just killed.

The location says, "Gravesite of John Hays, Lake View Cemetery." Under that, Kal writes: They say Archangel Michael will protect you if you ask him. I don't believe in angels, but it's a good statue. Maybe there's more to Ohio than a burning river.

But on these days of brightness... Shall the dead intrude?

CHAPTER TWENTY-FOUR

Hanami

The camp emails me a video of my presentation, and I forward it to my dad. He writes back right away about being proud and that we'd talk about the money stuff later and that he loves me. I was unpacked and in my room when the family rolled in from their trip. I had hung the kimono over my bed, on the wall opposite Cas A.

My mom stared at my haircut and I thought she was going to ask me why on earth I would do such a thing but she said, "I like it."

We hugged and meant it.

"I missed you, Julia."

"I missed you too, Mom."

She asked if I had won and I told her no, a boy made a flywheel.

She asked me about the kimono, and I told her I had met a girl from Tokyo and traded my entire wardrobe for it.

Is it possible my whip-smart mother never knew I didn't go to STEM camp?

Is it possible that, impressive as Kal's flywheel was, and unpracticed as my presentation was, I *did* win the prize?

Is it possible that with one phone call from Cabbage to my father my obscenely huge bill at the Hay-Adams was paid and never discussed again?

Is it possible that nothing happens all year and then one day a boy appears sleeping at the Vietnam Memorial and girl appears in a kimono texting and everything changes?

Yes, it is possible. Not probable but possible.

And is it possible that Clover Adams, wife of the author of one of the most famous biographies ever written, killed herself with photography chemicals and was never mentioned by her husband in his famous book? Is it possible she haunts the house she never got to move into, opening and closing locked doors, asking, "What do you want?"

For everything that I can't believe happened that really did, I pretend one thing *did* happen that really didn't. I heard a ghost at the Hay-Adams say, "What do you want?"

I thought for a long time about what I wanted, and then I thought of this: If I can be so changed by a girl who lived a thousand years ago, I can change a girl a thousand years from now. I'm not myself over and over again, or even a star waiting to implode or explode. I am the opposite of doomed.

At night I dream of dying stars and Mike Kovac. Sometimes I'm his backseater, our plane filled with heroin. I say, *Are you sure this is what we're supposed to be doing?* and he says, *By order of the U.S. Government*, and looks back at me, white T-shirt, aviator sunglasses, the smile of a believer. I say, *Did you know how much President Lincoln loved John Hay? He had a way of keeping the president's spirits up when there was only war and heartbreak.*

Out walking Avi, I see Mother and his wife in front of their house. He's holding the car door open for her as she gets in. He catches my eye and I smile but don't stop. They look like they're dressed to go out to dinner or a party and maybe he wouldn't want to talk about the things we might talk about.

The cherry trees do bloom. I take the Metro to Smithsonian Station. I walk down Independence Avenue to the Tidal Basin, sit underneath a bursting Yoshino tree and look out across the water at the crowds of people on the steps of the Jefferson Memorial practicing the ancient art of *hanami.*

We have an elaborate picnic. Nearly everyone is here, Clover and William Sturgis Bigelow, John and Clara Hay, Amayashi and Harukoshi, Tomoko and Kal and me.

Gratitude, Debt, Love

Lucy Scalzo, Robert Scalzo, Chris Scalzo, each in your own way never let me fall.

Leah Roberts, hours and hours of work, faith, belief.

Clare Girton, first and last reader.

Tomi Landis, what a surprise to discover the story in my head matched the one in your heart.

Judy Giannotti, Chuck Morrell, Marcella Smith, early advocates.

Gentle readers Peter Leonard, Vince Bzdek, Kelsey French, Liz Wieser, Maria Petaros, Barbara Noguera, Deborah Johnson, Linda Mallon, T. Miller, Kara Edwards, Julie Waterman, Meg Girton, Steve Dolge, Janet Zwick, Diana Rojas, Lila Weitzner, Mark Finkelpearl, Rue Zitner, Max Finkelpearl, Talia Zitner, Celia Byrne, Erik Kvalsvik, Gracene Sirianno, Molly Baker, Jeff Freel, Kara Parmelee, Tina Raisig, Pamela Weiss, Jeff Pesot, Margaret Hutton, Claire O'Brien, Stephen Roese, John Kelly, Hunter Bennett, Julie Maner, Michelle Dolge, Ken Bryant, Bill Clifford, Adam Buckman, Ainsley Phillips.

Steve Campbell, this incredible cover.

Nita Congress, keen-eyed and kind copy editor and designer.

DMV Women Writers, open-hearted and encouraging, thank you, Susan Shreve and Mary Kay Zuravleff.

Susan Shreve, again, for welcoming me into your studio and your wisdom. Alexandra Zapruder, for gravity and levity, Margaret Hutton, for clarity, Neroli Lacey, for practicality and poetry.

About the Author

Laura Scalzo lives in Washington, D.C., with her husband, two children, politicians of varying reliability, and the poets who came before her. She believes no matter how dreary the outlook, there will be a way, and in the power of storytelling and blossoming cherry trees. This is her first novel.

CPSIA information can be obtained
at www.ICGtesting.com
Printed in the USA
LVHW011438110319
610221LV00003B/542/P